HELL HATH NO FURY

HELL HATH NO FURY

NEW EDITION

PEGGY CHRISTIE

Dragon's Roost Press

Printed in the United States of America

Print ISBN 978-1-956824-34-6

Digital ISBN 978-1-956824-35-3

Dragon's Roost Press

2470 Hunter Rd.

Brighton, MI 48114

thedragonsroost.biz

DEDICATION

A big thanks to Dragons Roost Press for allowing me to put my mutated child back out into the world (again) with a couple (more) odd new growths that I probably should have had my dermatologist inspect first.

CONTENTS

Secretary's Day   1
Cabin Fever   35
Another Day in Paradise   53
Mother Knows Best   63
Mulligan   65
Fester   67
Reborn   77
Bad Touching   85
Earl   105
It's Not What You Think   109
A Rose by Any Other Name   121
Here There Be Monsters   133
The Lonely Corridor   141
Too Soon   161
Keeping Up With the Joneses   165
Don't Be a Dummy   177
I've Got a Secret   187
Manah Made Evil   191
Black Rain   207
Honor Thy Mother   213
Family Time   223
Driver's Ed   235
Endings   245
Publication History   247

About the Author   249
Also by Peggy Christie   251
Dragon's Roost Press   253

"**M**s. Phillips? We need to have a little talk."

Linda Phillips sighed, picked up her steno pad, and walked into Mr. Anderson's office. She closed the door behind her. Heaven forbid anyone should find out what 'having a little talk' was really all about. She sat down and looked up at him, waiting for the bomb to drop.

"Linda, it seems my report for the 1st quarter sales budget has been, uh, misplaced. Since you were the last one to work on it, you must have lost it.

Fortunately, for all involved, I assured the Executive Director that you would retype the report and have it on my desk by 11:00am."

Linda looked at her watch and grimaced. It was 9:55am. She had exactly one hour and five minutes to retype the eight-page budget spreadsheet. Mr. Anderson cleared his throat nervously and played with his tie. Linda clenched her jaw and glared at him. Her jaw muscles bunched and unbunched as she reined in her anger.

It wouldn't help to get mad. It wouldn't make a

difference if she pointed out that at five o'clock last night, she put the report directly in his hands. It didn't matter to him because he never made mistakes. She did. She always lost the report, spilled coffee on his keyboard, or erased the whole presentation ten minutes before a meeting.

That, of course, was not the truth. The truth was simply this: Gary Anderson was an asshole. He was born an asshole and he'd die an asshole. The man could not find his dick with a flashlight and a map. The only two things in this life that he ever did very well were taking the credit and placing the blame. It was because of his brilliance that the client accepted the proposal and earned the company an extra two billion dollars in revenue. It was because of someone else entirely that the proposal fell apart and went swirling down the toilet.

Linda remembered the days before Gary Anderson. Carl Wright was the Account Manager then and she was his Secretary. She didn't quibble over the title of Secretary or Assistant because she was happy. Mr. Wright always treated her well. He asked her if she wanted coffee when he was getting some for himself. If she was swamped with work, he was perfectly capable of making copies for himself, even the two-sided kind with staples. He remembered her birthday, her work anniversary, and even Secretary's Day.

Mr. Wright had worked for the company for 18 years. He was respected and well-liked by everyone. He had a great head for business and was a genius at putting people at ease. But, because of some botched pitch for new business, headed up by Gary Anderson coincidentally, Mr. Wright was fired and sent on his merry way. Linda cried the day he left, thinking things would never be the same around the office without him. The next day, when Mr. Anderson took over, she knew the good old days were gone forever.

Linda remembered Gary Anderson's first day as Account Manager as if it were yesterday. He came strutting into the office like a peacock rattling his feathers for a peahen's loving attentions. He called a department meeting that afternoon to spell out how "Gary's Team" would be structured and how things were going to be "different from now on." They would all work together. Everyone would have a say, a voice. No one was insignificant. He would take care of them and everyone would get the credit when a job was done well. "There's no 'I' in Team, is there?" That was one of Gary's favorite sayings. Of course, after the team got to know him a little better, they realized that there may not be an 'I' in team, but there definitely was a 'me' and that's all that Gary Anderson was interested in.

That was a little over a year ago. Since then, Linda had been ignored, denied vacation time, and pushed aside. Her ideas were always laughed at, her voice silenced on more than one occasion. Not by "the team" of course but by the leader himself. Gary Anderson looked at Linda as a necessary evil. He couldn't type a presentation or even make copies by himself without destroying something.

Linda was his link to the finished product. Once the work was completed, when the presentation or budget report was polished to a high shine, Gary swooped in and stole all the glory—from everyone. As far as Gary was concerned, Linda was just a glorified coffee maker with exceptional typing skills.

After she finished retyping the budget report, and other documents that had mysteriously disappeared, Mr. Anderson poked his head out of his office. "Ms. Phillips? We need to have a little talk."

Glancing up from her computer screen, Linda nodded. She saved her work and walked into Mr. Anderson's office.

Closing the door behind her, she prepared for the worst—again.

"Ms. Phillips, it seems someone has broken the copy machine because the original, and only, copy of the marketing presentation was destroyed in it this morning. Now, I know it wasn't your fault, because you were retyping the report you lost earlier. However, you will need to re-create the presentation before the end of the day tomorrow."

Linda frowned. "But, Mr. Anderson, don't you remember? I'm taking tomorrow off to go visit my sister."

"Well, I don't want you to miss out on that. I guess this will need to be done before you leave tonight."

"But Mr. Anderson...."

"Good. That's settled then. Now, you better get back to work. You've got a lot to finish up."

"Yes, sir." Linda muttered. She quietly closed his door and sat back in her cube. She leaned over and laid her head on the desk. After a few minutes, she began to thump her forehead in a quiet rhythm of frustration against the cool surface of her desk. Sitting up, she sighed and turned to her computer. The little clock in the corner noted 2:57pm. She grabbed the mouse and clicked. Nothing happened. She clicked it a few more times and just as she's was about to rip it out of the computer, a little message window popped up: "Systems Error. Retry? Reboot? Cancel?" She clicked on "Retry" and got the same message. Clicking on "Cancel", the message popped up again. "Of course," she groaned.

As she rebooted her computer, Linda looked up to see Mr. Anderson walking past in his coat and hat. "Good night, Linda. I'm all caught up on my work so I thought I'd cut out early. Enjoy your visit with your sister. See you on

Monday morning." As he breezed out the front door to the elevators, Linda gave him the finger.

After an exhausting and miserable weekend, Linda shuffled into work Monday morning. She'd had a huge fight with her sister on Saturday night about... well, what didn't they fight about? It started with whether to have pizza or hamburgers for dinner and ended with her sister accusing her of not spending enough time with their mom at the nursing home. Linda stomped out of her sister's house and drove back home. Halfway there, while fuming over the whole ordeal, she almost fell victim to a crater-sized pothole, gaping in the middle of the road like the toothless maw of some asphalt beast. Of course when she swerved to avoid that, she scraped her car along the steel barrier to her right, causing sparks to fly through the air like confetti. At least it was still drivable, albeit scarred.

Monday plugged along at its usual tortoise pace. At noon, Mr. Anderson announced he was taking a long lunch, to celebrate his glorious victory over signing up some new business that morning with his brilliant marketing proposal (never mind that he did none of the research, writing, or presenting of said proposal).

Around two thirty, he stumbled back to work, slurred a greeting to Linda, and locked himself in his office.

At about three forty five, one of the other secretaries, Cathy, went home with the flu. Cathy's boss, the Creative Director, asked Linda if she could help type up a presentation that needed to be ready for an 8:00am meeting the following morning. Of course, she'd be happy to help.

Yes, she understood that she wouldn't get out of here until later this evening. Fine. Great. No problem.

At 7:30, Linda was packing up her bag and getting ready to go home. She's seen neither hide nor hair of Mr. Anderson since 2:30 that afternoon. She knocked softly on his office door.

"Mr. Anderson?" She rapped a little louder this time. "Mr. Anderson, are you all right?"

She heard a grunt and groan, a snort, the sound of papers sliding off the desk, and a loud whump. After a few mumbled curses and some more banging, a disheveled Mr. Anderson opened his door. Clearing his throat, he looked bleary- eyed at Linda.

"Yes, Ms. Phillips. What is it?"

"I was just concerned about you, Mr. Anderson. You haven't been out of your office since early this afternoon. I just wanted to make sure..."

"What time is it?"

Linda looked down at her watch. "It's seven thirty, Mr. Anderson."

"Damn! I'm late for my dinner party with the client. I've got to get going!"

He lurched sideways to grab his coat and briefcase. Pushing Linda out of the way, he stumbled down the hall. Shaking her head in disgust, Linda closed up his office and headed out the door behind him.

As Linda walked to the parking garage, Mr. Anderson had already made it up to the sixth level where he had parked his silver 1997 Cadillac Seville. With shaking hands he tried several times to fit the key in the door lock before he remembered he had a remote entry system on this car. He depressed the button and a soft "bleep" sounded as the alarm shut off and the doors unlocked. He yanked open the door and threw his coat and briefcase onto the passenger seat. He knocked his forehead on the roof as he plunged into his car.

He took a quick inventory of his appearance in the rearview mirror. He looked awful. His eyes were blood shot and droopy. A red welt rose on the skin where he had just bumped his head. His suit was crumpled and smelled of cigarette smoke and whiskey. His hair was sticking up in back where he had fallen asleep in his chair. He spit on his fingers to wet his hair into submission, just like his mother did when he was five years old to make him presentable for church.

After getting his hair under reasonable control, he checked his breath.

Grimacing at the smell of sour liquor and stale cigarettes, he dug around his glove compartment for anything to cover that stench. His fingers closed over a single piece of chewing gum. He didn't know what flavor and didn't care. He unwrapped it as quickly as his shaking hands could manage. He crammed the stick into his mouth and bit down. The stale gum cracked and splintered into his mouth. As he worked on softening the gum, he smoothed his hands over his suit. Well, it's not going to get any better than this.

He took one last glimpse in the mirror, cringed, and started the car. He threw the car into reverse and pounded on the gas. With squealing brakes, he avoided crashing into a red Geo by mere inches. He took a deep breath, let it out in a curse, and slammed the car into drive grinding his foot into the accelerator. Driving like a condemned man escaping the gallows, he tore around the first corner to approach level five. The parking garage was actually quite long so he had a couple hundred yards of straightaway before he needed to turn again to reach the next level. He fumbled for his seatbelt, muttering to himself about how this was all Peter's fault.

Peter convinced him, no, made him drink those last three or four whiskey shots. Sure it was to celebrate his great work on some marketing proposal or whatever it was. Gary wasn't interested in the particulars. It was Peter's fault that he got so drunk he fell asleep in his office. And why hadn't Linda checked on him sooner? She should have come in and woken him up. It was her fault that he was late now. He was just going to have to have a little talk with her.

The parking garage was built like most others in the downtown area. Two center lanes allowed two-way traffic to enter and exit the structure. The single, one-way lanes wound along the east and west sides of the garage and connected back to the center at each level. Elevator banks and the stairwells were located in enclosed partitions at the southwest and northeast corners of the building. Gary was speeding down the outside lane towards the elevator on Level Five.

Adjacent to the elevators, the lane ended in a putty-grey cement wall, which was the outer wall of the garage, forcing a driver to turn right to advance down to the next parking level. As Gary approached the turn, he was thinking of what to do with Linda. She was so irresponsible. How many times did she have to retype a presentation because of her thoughtlessness? Well, he was just going to have a little... Too late, he saw her step out from the partition in front of his speeding car. Gary Anderson was going to have more than a little talk with Linda Phillips. He was going to kill her.

As Linda walked out of the elevator to Level Five, she was digging through her purse. She couldn't seem to find her damned keys. It wasn't really surprising.

After a horrible weekend with her sister and extra hours at work today, nothing could make her feel worse. She also felt guilty about the fight with her sister. She had to think of something to make it up to her. They never could stay mad at each other for very long. Even when they were kids growing up on their parent's farm in Petersburg, Illinois, they never stayed angry at each other past suppertime. After a hearty meal, with ice cream for dessert, they were giggling in each other's arms, usually trying to determine who was the reigning champion of their nightly tickle torture session.

Linda smiled to herself at the memory. A little giggle escaped her lips, making her sound like that long-ago girl, romping around on the living room floor, trying to get her sister to scream "uncle". Her hand finally closed around the cold metal of her key ring and she shook it in the air in triumph.

"Ah-ha!" she shouted as she walked toward her car. A bright light flashed in her eyes and she turned to her right, staring down the headlights of a 1997 silver Cadillac.

Time seemed to come to a halt, as if she were moving through molasses while wearing lead boots. In mere seconds, like a cliché, her life flashed through her mind: the summers in Petersburg with her family, her first pet—an English Setter named Buster, her first kiss, the first time she'd made love, her father's funeral, watching her mother waste away from MS.

As the tears began to well up in her eyes, as the anger and disappointment at dying in this garage in this way was crushing her heart with despair, as she heard her inner voice screaming 'IT'S NOT FAIR!', she glanced down at her keys. A bittersweet smile curled her lips. *I guess I won't be needing these after all*, she thought to herself. Then she took a trip where there were no more tears, no more regrets. Just darkness.

Gary Anderson sat staring at the wall. It had all happened so fast. He shook his head and placed his hands over his eyes, like a small boy who is playing hide and seek and must count to 100 before he can seek for his hidden friends. He slowly spread his fingers apart, peering through them towards the garage wall. Maybe if he couldn't really see it, it wasn't really there. It never really happened at all.

But it had happened. He pulled his hands away from his eyes. A large wet blotch dripped down the wall in front of him. Anyone walking by would have thought someone threw a bucket of red paint on the wall. For what purpose, that hypothetical someone could not determine. On closer inspection this person would have found small bits of brains and bone clinging to the wall within the red paint, only then realizing that it wasn't paint at all. It was blood. Linda Phillips' blood.

Linda Phillips' brains and skull and blood splattered all over that damnable wall, for all to see.

He squeezed his eyes shut and clamped his hands over his head. He started talking to himself. "Okay, Gary. Get a grip. It's not your fault. It was just an accident. Just an accident, all right? You never saw her coming. She just stepped right out in front of you. She should have been watching. She should have been paying attention. It was really her fault, don't you see?"

He did see. It wasn't his fault at all. He glanced up and studied Linda's body.

Her broken figure was fully illuminated in his headlights. He tilted his head to the side, studying her, like a dog that sees its reflection in a mirror and can't quite figure out how that other dog has gotten into his house.

He replayed the accident in his mind. He had slammed on his brakes, although not to keep from hitting Linda. By the time he saw her it was too late. He had to stop the car from being crushed like a tin can against the garage wall. After choking down his gum, he watched Linda's body as it sailed into the air and hit the wall with a sickening thud that he could hear even over the screeching tires. She had hit the wall so hard she bounced off of it into a heap of twisted arms and legs a few feet from its base. Gary couldn't help thinking she looked like a paper cut-out doll that someone had crumpled up and thrown over their shoulder without a care.

But Gary cared. He cared big time. He cared about getting caught and going to jail. He pictured the trial, the judge, the jury. They wouldn't believe it was an accident. They'd think he did it on purpose. They'd think he was a callous, cold-hearted monster that mowed down this pretty young woman in the prime of her life. It'd be a death sentence for sure. Even if he was spared capital punishment, he still couldn't bear the thought of being locked up in jail with large hairy criminals who'd like nothing more than to have a 'crack' at breaking in the new guy.

He can't get caught. He just can't. Panic seized Gary by the throat and squeezed. His heart pounded at a marathon pace. He ran his hands through his sweat-dampened hair. While frantically chewing on his nails his eyes darted around garage to see if anyone was watching, waiting to point their fingers and start screaming bloody murder. An idea slowly blossomed in his mind. He gnawed on his right thumbnail a little longer as he tried to work out all the kinks and possible problems. It might work. It could work. It had to work.

Gary pulled into an empty space and cut the engine. Once he was out of his car, he picked up Linda's purse and looked for her keys. He couldn't find them. Damn! He scratched his head and looked around, thinking they may have been thrown from her bag, but he couldn't see them anywhere. As he stood up and thought about where they could possibly be, his jaw dropped slack and his eyes bulged in fear. Trembling, he glanced over his shoulder towards Linda's body. There, clutched in her right hand in a death grip, were Linda's keys.

With a grimace of fear contorting his features, Gary slowly stepped toward Linda's body. As he approached her limp form, Gary whimpered. He could see the blood pooling out from various wounds on her body but mostly from her skull.

Her green eyes were wide and staring, as if she were, at this moment, seeing that tunnel of light that supposedly leads on to everlasting peace and happiness. Her legs, specifically her knees, were bent the wrong way. Gary thought it might be his imagination, but he could almost make out the markings of his Caddy's grill imprinted onto her legs.

Just as he was about to go insane with fear, he clamped his eyes shut and slapped his face several times—hard. He took a few deep breaths and slowly opened his eyes. It was almost as if a veil had been pulled down over his features. His eyes were blank and glazed and he looked impassively over at Linda's prone figure. He walked briskly up to her, bent down, and gripped the keys in her hand. When they didn't come loose right away, his features contorted with fear, but only for a moment. Then the veil fell back into place and he grabbed her hand and wrenched the keys from her grip. He stepped back from the body and walked over to the only car still parked on this side of the structure. As he assumed, it was Linda's car. He slid the keys into the trunk lock and popped it open.

Luckily, the trunk was relatively empty. There was an ice scraper, windshield fluid, and a plastic shopping bag from some trendy store in the city that was filled with old sweaters and sweatshirts. He pushed it all toward the back, except for the bag of clothes, to make room for Linda. He took the bag out of the trunk and walked back over to her, leaving the keys in the trunk lock. Just as he was about to pick her up, her eyes blinked once.

He faltered, staring wide-eyed at her for a moment. Then he pinched his eyes shut, shook his head and bent down so he was face to face with her. He put his nose right up to hers and held it there for several minutes. When she didn't blink again, he figured he had imagined it. He leaned over, pushing his arms beneath her and gingerly scooped her up into his embrace. Anyone walking by might have thought he was helping a friend who had drunk too much at a party. Or perhaps they would be mistaken for lovers, sneaking away for a secret tryst at some local motel.

He moved quickly to the open trunk and gently laid the body down. Her skirt had pushed up over her knees and Gary modestly pulled it back into place. He walked back over to the bag of clothes and grabbed a couple of the bulky sweatshirts. He used them to mop up the blood on the wall. At first the blood just swirled around, the sweatshirts not doing a good job of absorbing the fluid. But then the splotch got smaller and smaller until there was just a slight pink tinge in the concrete. It wasn't completely gone but he didn't have time to do a more thorough job.

He threw the ruined sweatshirts in the open trunk and grabbed some of the sweaters to sop up the blood on the floor. This was even more difficult to clean because there was an actual puddle of the stuff and it was quickly soaking into the concrete. He used all the remaining clothes in the bag to clean up the mess. There was a round dark stain left in the concrete but there was nothing else he could do, except hope that no one would notice it.

He packed all the blood soaked clothes back in the plastic shopping bag. He was about to close the trunk lid when he looked at his bloodied hands. He would leave fingerprints all over the place if he wasn't more careful. He leaned in and grabbed Linda's coat. He wiped his hands clean as best he could and studied them closely. It would have to do for now. Reaching up, he used the sides of his hands and then his elbows to close the trunk lid.

Sliding in behind the wheel of Linda's car he thought he heard a small 'thump' come from the trunk. Pausing, he leaned his head out the door and listened. Hearing nothing more he pulled the door closed and started the engine. He figured the noise was all in his head, just like the vision of Linda blinking her eyes right before he picked her up. Just a little stress-induced hallucination. That was all.

The part of Gary's brain that hadn't subsided into madness was screaming at him. Screaming to let him know that what he was doing was wrong, evil, and inhuman.

Gary, think! Call the police. Turn yourself in and they'll be lenient. It was only an accident. Accidents happen every day. But if they find out what you're doing now, it'll only make things worse. Gary? GARY!

But Gary couldn't hear that voice anymore. He started to hum a little tune he remembered from childhood, one his mother used to sing to get him to fall asleep. "Rock-a-bye baby, on the treetop. When the wind blows the cradle will rock. When the bough breaks, the cradle will fall. And down will come baby, cradle and all." Inside, the sane Gary was still screaming.

Gary exited the parking garage in Linda's car and headed south of the city.

He recalled that there was a large man-made lake about five or ten miles out of town. If all went well, he could arrive at the lake, dump the car and Linda's corpse, sneak back to the garage to retrieve his own vehicle, and be home long before dawn. He might even be able to get in a few hours' sleep before returning to work in the morning. Gary reached over and flipped on the radio. A local rock station came blaring out at him and he winced. He quickly scanned through the channels until the sweet strains of country music poured into the car. He grinned like the Cheshire cat and started swaying back and forth to the music.

Within 15 minutes, a sign popped up on the right: GREENSIDE LAKE - NEXT EXIT. Gary turned off the radio to concentrate on his driving. He flipped on the turn signal (wouldn't do to be pulled over now for a minor traffic violation) and exited the highway. The ramp curved around to the right, then to the left, and ended at a T-section. Another sign told him that Green side Lake was one mile due north so he'd best be turning right if he wanted to reach it. Technically it didn't say that but Gary liked his interpretation of the brown and white sign with an arrow pointing north better that what the highway commission erected.

As he approached the lake he searched for a dark and secluded area for the deposit. Most of the houses built on Greenside Lake were over on the far west side with a few dotting the north, leaving the east bank empty except for the lone wooden dock jutting out into the water. Although the road curved around and headed toward the north and west banks, Gary stopped in the small parking area on the east side, where there were no lights and, more importantly, no people.

Shutting off the engine and lights, Gary sat behind the wheel for a few minutes, surveying the area. There were a few lights on in the houses across the way and the three major docks on that side were flooded with light. But since it was a Monday night, everyone was inside watching the news, eating dinner, or rounding up the kids to get their homework finished. That was good. He was hoping for no interference from anyone or anything. He couldn't have anyone find out about this...situation. He drummed his fingers on the steering wheel. His eyes darted back and forth. He licked his lips, which suddenly felt as dry as a dirt road in ninety-five degree heat. Seeing no one, he finally got out of the car.

Walking around to the trunk, he took one last glance about. The night was black and silent. He popped the trunk and stared at Linda's body. As he was about to pull her out, he leaned in for a closer look. He was planning on putting her body in the front seat and just rolling the car into the water. However, if her body was found before the water could bloat away any incriminating evidence, it would look like someone had hit her with their car and dumped her body. Granted, that was exactly what was happening but Gary didn't want anyone to know that. He wanted it to look like an attack, like a mugging or a rape. Gary grimaced as his gag reflex kicked in at the thought of having to make Linda's corpse look like a rape victim. Maybe a botched robbery attempt or a full-out robbery/murder would suffice. Yes, that would work nicely.

First, he had to go through her purse and coat to get all of her valuables. Rummaging through her purse, he discovered $24 in cash and two credit cards in her wallet. He took it all. The only other objects he found were a half roll of breath mints, a tube of lipstick, and a hair brush. He popped one of the mints into his mouth as he looked through the pictures in her wallet.

She only had two. One was an old photo of a couple in their mid-fifties standing in front of the Empire State Building, smiling and waving. Gary assumed these were Linda's parents. He seemed to remember something about her father being dead. Or was it her mom? The other picture was of a young woman in her late twenties or early thirties. She had long wavy red hair and bright green eyes, like Linda. Actually, this woman and Linda could have been twins. This must be her sister. What was her name? Karen? Carol? Gary shrugged and tossed the wallet back into the purse.

He turned to Linda's body and searched the pockets. He found nothing there. Next, he surveyed Linda's injuries. Most of them looked like someone took a bat or other blunt instrument to her. That would go along with the mugging and attack idea. There wasn't much he could do about the Caddy's grill imprint on her legs. He just hoped the water would have enough time to erase those bruises. He tossed the purse on top of her body and nodded in satisfaction. Everything looked in order.

He slammed the trunk closed and opened the driver's door. He quickly wiped down the interior with a handkerchief before he stuck the keys in the ignition and turned it over just enough to put the car into neutral. He got out and started to push. Grunting, he didn't realize how difficult it was to push several thousand pounds of metal and plastic. His face turned purple with the strain. Just as he began to think the car wasn't going to cooperate, it slowly rolled forward.

He picked up his pace and jogged with the car. As it came within two feet of the waterline, he gave one last hard shove and jumped clear of the car.

He stood back and watched the car slowly but surely sink into the lake. He stood with a small smile on his face as the water churned and bubbled up over the hood, the windshield, and the doors. Finally, when only the ass-end was sticking up, Gary had a crazy notion that the car would stop sinking and bob up and down for a while, just like in the movies. And then, as he would begin to panic, there would be a loud hissing and gurgling sound as the car finally sank into the depths of the water. In reality the car only bobbed for a few seconds before the lake sucked it down. He was almost disappointed.

He turned away from the water and looked back up toward the highway. He had a long walk ahead of him before it was really all over. He looked down at his watch. It was eight-thirty. He made a small surprised squeak in the back of his throat. It had only been one hour since this whole mess began. He figured it'd be a couple of hours of walking before he got back to his car, thirty minutes to get back home, and another half an hour on top of that to get the car cleaned up. Smiling, he calculated his arrival at home to be between midnight and 1:00am. That would give him plenty of time to get a decent night's sleep and be all refreshed for work

Tuesday morning. Taking one last look over his shoulder, just to be sure the car hadn't popped back up to the surface, which it hadn't, he smiled to himself and started his long trek back home.

His calculations were slightly off. He didn't get back to the parking garage until after midnight. It was almost as if the gods were purposely trying to impede his every move, as if they wanted him to get caught. Since he didn't want to be seen walking along the highway shoulder, he'd had to trudge through the weeds, tall grass, and garbage strewn along the service drive. Several times he had tripped over discarded tires hidden among the overgrowth. Once he got his foot caught in a greasy fast-food chicken bucket and had to sit down in order to pry it off with his hands. Of course, he sat right in the middle of a shallow but rancid sludge puddle and now reeked of oil, urine, and something akin to rotting meat.

As he was skulking along in the shadows, a police car came cruising down the service drive. Just as its headlights were about to wash over him, he dove into the tall grass on his right, smacking headfirst into the post of a speed limit sign. His vision swam for a moment and bright bursts of white light flashed before his eyes. Luckily, the police car turned down a side street and the officers did not see Gary before he lost consciousness.

Gary was dreaming about his high school sweetheart. It

was the Junior Spring Dance and he and Mary Weathers were making out under the bleachers at the football field. Gary's hands were exploring Mary's firm young body eagerly even as she was exploring his. He plunged his hands into her long wavy red hair...wait. Mary had short blonde hair. He frowned in his dream even as he embraced her. His hands touched something wet and sticky and he pulled back in horror as he stared at the blood covering his hands.

When he looked back up to Mary, the first thing he noticed was the rumpled trench coat. His eyes took in the torn pantyhose and the bloodied and broken knees bending the wrong way. Shaking with horror, he forced his gaze up to Mary's face. Only it wasn't Mary anymore. Linda Philips was staring back at him, her finger raised, pointing in accusation at her murderer. When she opened her mouth to speak, water and muck dribbled out and stained the front of her blouse. Suddenly, she was soaking wet from head to toe. Her body distorted until it was bloated and rotting, green with algae and death, as if she had been trapped in the lake for weeks instead of mere hours. She waddled toward him, holding her arms wide for an embrace. As she leaned in for a kiss, her blackened tongue searching for his, he awoke with a scream.

As he swatted and flailed his hands, Gary opened his eyes and realized that he wasn't kissing the rotting corpse of Linda Philips. There was, however, a large St. Bernard lapping at his face and drooling all over his suit. He pushed the dog away in disgust, wiping his hands over his mouth. He then noticed a leash attached to the dog and followed it up to look into the face of a small wide-eyed boy, probably 10 or 11, judging by the gangly arms and legs.

"Gee, mister. Are you all right?"

Gary coughed. "Yes, I'm fine."

"You rammed yourself into that pole pretty good. You'll have a nice big goose egg on your forehead by tomorrow morning."

Gary growled in despair, rubbing his head. "Yep. Probably. What time is it, do you know?"

"About 9:45pm. I saw you dive for cover when that cop car came up the drive."

Gary stopped cold. He slowly looked up at the boy.

"Then I heard the pole vibrating," the boy continued. "Even from where I was standing I could hear it. Like I said, you rammed it pretty good. Then Coop took off...that's my dog here, Coop. Coop took off and came running over to you. Why are you hiding from the police?"

Gary tried to stand but the world pulled a three-sixty on him and he collapsed back to the ground. His voice was a little weak. "I wasn't hiding from the police. I just couldn't see where I was going and I ran into the pole and knocked myself out, that's all. My car broke down and I was..."

But the boy was shaking his head. "No, you dove into that sign. I saw it." He started pulling on Coop and backing away, towards the side street and away from Gary. "I saw it. C'mon, Coop. Let's go get the police. Let's go, Coop."

The boy was yanking on the leash but Coop was determined to keep guard over Gary. He smiled and spoke sweetly to the dog, hoping to ease the boy's fears, and to keep him from running.

"Good dog, Coop. Good boy. You see, son? If I am such a bad guy, why is your dog being so nice to...." Coop's low growl hit Gary's ears and he froze in place.

"Ah-ha!" the boy yelled. "I knew it. My dog knows a crook when he sees one. C'mon, Coop!"

Finally the boy was able to pry his dog from guard duty

and went running down the street, yelling at the top of his voice.

"Help! Help! Somebody help!"

Lights were snapping on all down the street as the boy ran, following him like they were attached to those gadgets that turned the lights on or off whenever you clapped. Instead of clapping, though, you turned them on by having an 11 year old boy scream bloody murder.

Gary lurched to his feet and stumbled away. After the ground finally stopped swaying beneath him, he was able to run in a straight line and make better progress. From only a few miles away he heard a siren wailing. Damn those cops! Why couldn't they have patrolled after he'd passed by? He wouldn't have knocked himself out and that whiney little brat wouldn't have seen him. And what the hell was that kid doing out this late with his dog anyway?

Silently cursing everyone and everything for getting him into this mess, he ran on. The siren grew louder. He looked back and could see the flashing red and blue lights across the tops of the trees and between the houses. The lights also illuminated Coop running at top speed toward him.

Coop's jowls were flapping in the breeze, slobber was flying all around his face, and his teeth flashed large and sharp. A frightened whimper escaped Gary's lips and just as he turned forward again he ran into a chain link fence and was thrown to the ground. His breath whooshed out of him in one big 'oof' as he landed.

Sparing no time to blame whoever built the damned thing, he scrambled up the fence and went ass over applecart across the top. Just as he landed on his backside, Coop launched himself at the fence, bowing it towards Gary's face.

Coop snarled and barked, gnashing his teeth and spitting slobber all over Gary. He crab-walked backwards away from the hell hound and collapsed, panting and shaking. Knowing he had only minutes to spare to escape, Gary took a deep breath and rose to his feet. Almost as an afterthought, he turned back to Coop, lifted his suit coat and shook his fanny. This enraged the dog even further and he tried to jump up and over the fence. Luckily for Gary, the St. Bernard was much too large and the fence was too high. Giggling like a school boy, Gary ran off into the dark, leaving Coop to bark at the air.

After what seemed like an eternity, Gary finally reached the parking garage around twelve-thirty. Fortunately, no one was around at his hour. As he approached his car, he dug in his pants pocket for his keys. For one desperate moment, he thought he may have left them at the lake or dropped them after his wild run along the highway. He sighed with relief when he remembered they were in his suit coat. He dug them out, unlocked his car, and collapsed in the front seat. He thought he would never get there.

Ever since he had dumped Linda's body, it was one problem after another. Things had gone so smoothly up until that point. It was almost as if, right before he had rolled Linda's corpse into the lake, fate was still giving him a chance to turn back. He could do the right thing and go to the police. But since he chose the path of darkness and cowardice instead, fate, karma, the gods, or whatever the hell was out there was doing everything in its power to fuck him up.

Before he started the engine, he got out and surveyed the car. There was a slight dent in the grill but nothing extraordinary. The immediate problem was the blood. He had to get his car cleaned up. And, as he looked down at his rumpled, mud-soaked, blood-stained suit, he needed a good washing as well. His overcoat was still in the front seat so he laid it down on the driver's side before sitting down again. He got behind the wheel and started the car. Luckily he had a pass card to park in this garage so he didn't need to talk to or see any of the attendants, if there even were any working at this hour.

He pulled out of the garage and headed home. There was a coin car wash a mile or so from his house. He thought it might look a little odd if he started washing his car in his driveway in the middle of the night. Even for the coin operated car washes it might look a little strange, but not completely unheard of, to have a late night customer from time to time.

Sal's Car Wash came into view on his right. As he pulled into one of the empty slots, he noticed there was one other person here. He wasn't as likely to be noticed if anyone, particularly a cop, drove by. He had taken the stall farthest away from the other patron. As he reached over into his briefcase to retrieve his wallet, the other customer walked past the front of his car. Gary froze, watching the man as he took a passing glance toward Gary's vehicle. He audibly gulped, making that little clicking noise in the back of his throat that had suddenly gone very dry. The man kept on walking and Gary started to panic. After a few minutes, the man came back with a handful of quarters, counting through them to make sure he got the right amount of change. Gary breathed a sigh of relief. Apparently, the change machine was right next to the slot Gary chose.

Before Gary got out of his car to go get quarters for himself, he happened to glance down at his shirt. His jacket and shirt were soaked with blood. There was no way he could wash his car while he was covered in gore. He pulled his overcoat out from underneath him. It was dark blue, almost black. He pulled this on and buttoned it up to the collar. Looking down at himself, he could see no traces of blood. Smiling, he got out of his car and went to the change machine. He was whistling "A Spoonful of Sugar" as he waited for the machine to spit out his $5 in quarters.

By the time Gary pulled into his driveway, it was close to 2:00am. He parked his now clean and sparkling car into his garage and closed the door.

Exhausted, he dragged himself through the side entrance, into a narrow hallway, and stripped off his bloody clothes. He had a small storage cabinet here and from there he grabbed a garbage bag and carefully bagged up his soiled clothes, being sure not to smudge blood on anything. He threw everything in the bag, tied it up, and left it on the basement stairs. Once he had showered and cleaned up, he would take his clothes downstairs to the old stove and burn them.

He had inherited this house, which was built in the late 1800s, from his grandparents. It had one of those old potbellied stoves in the basement that was still in working order. Gary's grandparents would fire the old gal up when he was a kid because he loved the smell of the burning wood. He knew that if it wasn't for him, they would have thrown the thing away years ago. He whispered a quick 'thank you' to his grandparents' memory and went upstairs to shower.

Standing in front of the stove in the basement, Gary watched his clothes burn away into ash. Some of it was polyester that just melted into a gooey black ooze that stuck to the interior of the stove. Since it matched the color of the stove, it was not that noticeable. The smell, however, was horrendous. But he couldn't open the windows to air it out unless he wanted the whole neighborhood to reek. At the last minute he tossed in the garbage bag. Might as well burn it all, he thought. It couldn't make any more of a mess than that polyester-blend suit.

He watched the fire burn for a little while longer as he ran over the evening's events. From all that he could remember, even with the bump to the head, he had covered all his tracks. There weren't any bloody clothes or prints anywhere, the garage and his car were clean and his clothes were (almost) gone. And, most importantly, there was no body. Granted, that kid had run for the police. But Gary wasn't from that area and it was dark. The boy couldn't have gotten too good a look at him. Good thing dogs can't talk or Coop would have made sure his ass was in jail already. Gary mouth suddenly gaped with huge yawn. He rubbed his eyes and turned for the stairs. Glancing at a wall clock, he noticed it was three-fifteen. He could just get in about four hours of sleep before he had to get up for work. Not bad. Not bad at all.

Gary strolled into work a little early on Tuesday morning as if he didn't have a care in the world. "Just act innocent, and you'll be innocent," he murmured to himself. He breezed into his office, tossing his briefcase onto the chair opposite his desk. After hanging up his coat, he sat down at his desk and leaned back in his chair, kicking his feet up. After a minute or two of twiddling his thumbs, he was unsure of what to do next. He supposed coffee was in order to get the day going.

After sitting at his desk for another minute he realized

that Linda got him coffee every morning. He frowned down at his desk blotter as if puzzling out how he could enjoy his morning coffee without actually having to get it himself. His black mug sat alone on the corner of his desk. He picked it up and studied it, peering inside as if the coffee might be hiding in there. "Well," he said out loud to his office. "I guess I'll have to get my own coffee today."

He decided that it might look good for him if he pretended to look around for Linda, just in case someone was watching. He walked over to her cubicle and peeked in.

"Ms. Phillips?" he called out. Wiping his hand over his mouth to hide a tiny smile, he shrugged and spoke aloud. "Oh, well. Seems I'll have to get my own coffee this morning."

He walked out to the copier area, where there was not only a coffee machine, but also a water cooler and two vending machines, offering a variety of processed and additive filled foods to satisfy the most particular palate. The employees had dubbed it "The Gathering" after the popular role-playing game. As he was filling his coffee mug, Paul Kirtchner, the biggest suck-up of an employee next to Gary, walked up to him.

"Hey, Gar. Where were you last night? Mr. Carlson was looking all over for ya."

Gary could see the hungry glint in Paul's eyes. Paul had been gunning for Gary from the day they first met and was just waiting for something like this to gloat over. He also hated it when Paul called him 'Gar' and he knew it.

"Good morning, Paul. Yes, I've spoken with Mr. Carlson already. I came down with the flu late yesterday. I think Cathy must have given it to Linda and I caught it from her. As a matter of fact, Linda isn't in this morning so she must be home sick. She really needs to take better care of...

her....self...." Paul's brow furrowed in confusion. "Gar? You all right?"

Gary was staring off down the hall towards his office. Linda Phillips was standing outside her cubicle staring directly at Gary. She wasn't pointing at him, as in his dream. She was just standing there, looking at him, a puddle of water gathering at her feet. Gary's mouth dropped from a small 'oh' of surprise to a lengthened gape of fear. He took a few steps back and bumped into the coffee machine. Only when Paul finally snapped his fingers in front of Gary's eyes did he turn from the vision of Linda's soaking corpse. He blinked at Paul.

"Wha.....Did you day something, Paul?"

"Are you all right, Gar?"

"Oh, I'm fine. I just..." Gary turned to look down the hall again and Linda was gone. He shook his head. "I'm just feeling a little dizzy, that's all. Thanks."

He walked away, leaving Paul to stare after him with a puzzled look on his face. Before he locked himself inside his office, Gary realized that he told Paul he'd already spoken with Mr. Carlson about his absence from the client dinner last night. Gary sighed and walked down the hall before Paul had a chance to tell the old man he had lied.

When he was just a few doors down from Carlson's office, the door to the conference room on his right opened. Linda stepped right out in front of him and he bumped into her. But instead of the normal stumble and laughed apologies, Linda's body went sailing towards the wall, bounced off of it and came crashing down with a loud thud. A dark red splotch, that looked similar to red paint, dripped down the wall outside Mr. Carlson's office. Linda's broken and battered body lay crumpled in front of Carlson's door and when he walked out, Mr. Carlson stepped right over her as if she wasn't there. As he handed his secretary something to type, Mr. Carlson glanced over at Gary.

"There you are, Mr. Anderson. I've been meaning to talk to you about last night."

Gary just stood there staring at him in bug-eyed disbelief. He side-stepped to the right, blocking Linda's body from his view with Mr. Carlson's frowning face. He watched in horror as Mr. Carlson leaned on the wall, placing his left hand directly in the middle of the spatter of blood.

"Mr. Anderson, I'm concerned that you didn't make the dinner last night...."

But Gary was hardly hearing him. He watched in morbid fascination as Mr. Carlson stepped away from the wall and ran his now bloodied hand through his hair. He rubbed his nose and chin, spreading the blood all over his face and neck. As he made a pointing gesture, blood spattered in Gary's face and he flinched away. He could barely hear Mr. Carlson comment on how he was disappointed in him and how bad it looked for the company. All Gary could concentrate on was how Mr. Carlson was spreading the blood all over himself. He found it quite comical, in an over-the-edge-hysteria kind of way.

Just as he was started giggling, a hand peeked out and laid itself on Mr. Carlson's shoulder. With a lover's caress, the hand slid down and gripped his boss's upper arm. Slowly, Linda peered out from behind Mr. Carlson and glared at Gary. The giggle that was sitting in the back of his throat was crushed and swallowed. A bitter taste, like aspirin, slithered over his tongue and he grimaced. He shook his head back and forth and whimpered.

"Mr. Anderson?" Mr. Carlson stopped talking and

frowned with concern instead of anger at Gary. "What's the matter?"

Gary stammered a reply. "I....I'm sorry about l-l-last night, Mr. Carlson.

But I c-c-came down with the, uh, the flu last night and, uh..."

Linda wagged a finger at him and frowned, calling out his lie. Her arm shot out as she reached for him. Gary squeaked and lurched backwards, watching the spot over Mr. Carlson's shoulder. He shuddered.

"I'm, uh, I'm still not feeling very w-w-well. I'd like to go back to my office n-n-now."

Gary power-walked down the hall, glancing back over his shoulder every couple of steps. He tripped and sprawled to the floor. He scrambled up to his feet and continued walking. He stood outside his office door and looked back down the hall at Mr. Carlson. Linda was still wagging her finger at him. He whimpered in terror and slammed the door, locking it. Mr. Carlson frowned and looked over his shoulder. Seeing nothing, he glanced back down at Gary's office. He shook his head in confusion and disgust.

After a restless sleep, Gary returned to the office on Wednesday morning feeling frazzled and disjointed. His dreams were filled with images of green bloated corpses, lakes of blood, and his own death by various methods. One dream had him strapped onto the front bumper of his car while Linda drove it at a hundred miles per hour and rammed it into a cement wall. The next was of him trapped, shin- deep in lake muck, being sucked and pulled down into the earth. As he flailed his arms and tried to stop from being pulled under, Linda stood over him and laughed.

As he slumped into his chair, exhausted, he realized he was suffering from some kind of post-traumatic stress that was causing the bad dreams and the hallucinations. He wasn't sure he could keep up this charade. The flu excuse would only fly so far. He decided that he would try to avoid as many people as he could for today but after that, he better get back into the game. Yes, tomorrow he'd be better. As a matter of fact, he hadn't seen Linda yet today and that was a good sign. Maybe all those bad dreams helped work some of the stress out of his system.

Just then he looked up and saw Linda standing in his open door. He gulped and squeezed his eyes shut. He muttered a "She's Not Real" mantra over and over for a minute or two. When he opened them again, she was still standing there but she was more of a vague outline, a ghostly apparition. He mustered up his courage and walked over to her. As her eyes looked up into his and her eyebrows knitted together in a slight frown, he slammed the door in her face.

For the rest of the day, he only saw Linda twice. Once she was sitting at her desk, typing away, as a puddle of lake water pooled around her chair. He didn't get a look at her face, thankfully , just her ragged and cracked nails tapping away and smudging the keyboard with sediment. The second time was in the men's room. As he stood at the sink washing his hands, he saw her reflection in the mirror. She was standing behind him in front of the stall he'd just vacated. She was no longer wet or even bloody. She was dressed and ready as if it was the end of the working day and she was ready to go home, but wanted to check in with him one last time before leaving. He refused to look at her for more than a few seconds. When he turned around, she was gone. "I'm going to make it," he whispered to himself. "I'm going to make it." She didn't appear again for the rest of the day.

Thursday was relatively uneventful. He was no longer fazed by Linda's sudden appearances all over the office and his home. He got back into his old routine. He even voiced his concerns about Linda's whereabouts to Mr. Carlson and volunteered to find out where she was. After all, she'd been gone for three days with no word and there was no answer at her home. Mr. Carlson just shook his head and said he'd have personnel look into it.

"Linda sure is lucky to have such a caring supervisor like you, Gary." Gary half smiled as if embarrassed by the compliment. His stomach rolled over in a greasy flop and he shrugged to cover his guilt.

By Friday, the personnel department had been unable to locate Linda at her home and the Director of Human Resources, Susan Altman, had contacted Linda's sister, Carol. Carol had no idea where Linda was and hadn't heard from her since the previous weekend. She thanked Ms. Altman for her call and informed her that she would contact the police immediately. Gary found out all this over lunch with Susan on Friday afternoon. Susan had heard how concerned he was for Linda's well- being and wanted to keep him abreast of the latest happenings. Gary played his best 'aw-shucks' routine with all the relish he could muster. By the look on Susan's face, he had secured his innocence with her and therefore, the entire company, since Susan was the biggest gossip he'd ever encountered.

The weekend passed without incident. He had stopped seeing visions of Linda by Saturday morning. He was able to get through a dinner with friends on Saturday night without any panic attacks or gruesome hallucinations. He had done it. He beat her. He won.

Monday morning arrived and Gary practically floated into work. He'd tried not to look too complacent. After all, Linda was still missing. But he had a soft smile and wink for the ladies, and a hearty 'good morning' to all the gentlemen.

He stepped into his office and hung up his coat and hat. He grabbed his mug and headed for the coffee machine. There was a slight spring in his step as he sauntered up through the hallway and approached "The Gathering" area.

As he reached for the coffee pot, he noticed muddy fingerprints all over the counter. The plastic storage bin of individual packets of coffee, the filter bags, the pot, and the machine itself were covered in wet and dried muck. It looked as if someone had plunged their hands into a child's mud pie and then handled all the coffee equipment. A cold spike of fear lodged itself in his heart and his breath caught in his lungs. He looked down at the floor and saw muddy footprints leading away from the coffee machine back towards the offices. He shut his eyes and counted to ten. He opened his left eye, then his right. The prints were still there. He knew they definitely belonged to a woman as Gary noted dots of mud, signifying a woman's standard high heel, and the small dainty outline of a bare foot.

His mouth opened and closed like a fish out of water, gasping for breath. His hands fell numbly to his sides and his coffee mug went crashing to the floor, shattering into a hundred fragments. With his head down, he followed the trail of prints back down the hall, like an obedient slave, his mouth still gaping, his vocal chords working to find his voice. The footprints made a direct line to his office and disappeared behind the closed door. He reached for the handle, wetting his hand on the grime left there. He slowly pushed the door open.

Standing there, behind his behemoth maple desk, was Linda Phillips. She was soaking wet from head to toe. Her once shining red hair was hanging in ropes of muck and mud. The green in her irises had clouded over to a murky teal color and the whites were red from burst blood vessels. She was standing on legs that bent the wrong way, with the jagged ends of her tibias poking out through the skin of where her knees used to be. Her skin was mottled with blue-green blotches and sloughing off of her face and hands.

Her bony fingers were grasping his coffee mug, intact and empty. As she leaned over to place it on his desk, she opened her mouth. Brown water spewed out and into his mug, filling it to the brim. Looking up at him, a thin line of black sludge dribbled down her chin. She bared her brown-stained teeth at him in a smile and her blackened tongue licked her cracked and split lips. When she spoke, her voice croaked out from the shadows of a nightmare.

"Mr. Anderson, we need to have a little talk."

Gary was shaking his head back and forth, lost in a spiral of denial of his senses and acceptance of what was to come. This was no hallucination. This was no ghost. For the first time in his life, he was going to have to take responsibility for his mistakes. As his office door slowly creaked to a close behind him, Gary Anderson finally found his voice.

And screamed.

CABIN FEVER

Henry stood on the deck in his back yard and inhaled deeply. The sweet summer air cleansed his lungs and his mind. Two days into his sabbatical and already he could feel the tension and frustrations of the corporate world sliding away. He had at least six more months to enjoy this time off, before he needed to look for work again. He really wished he could retire but at 48, it was a bit too soon, particularly where his finances were concerned. After all, he did have a wife and two kids to support.

He and Cheryl had been married 20 years and had two daughters, Nicki and Angela, aged 10 and 8 respectively. Henry and Cheryl tried for 10 years to have kids but to no avail. They adopted the two girls once they realized they couldn't have children of their own. And he loved them more than anything in the world.

Nicki was bright and inquisitive, with shiny blonde hair and dark brown eyes. Angela was more reserved and shy, more often than not clinging to Cheryl's leg or hiding behind her skirt. But her copper hair and ice blue eyes were all that she needed to get the attention she did want.

Cheryl was tall and statuesque, with short brown hair and bright blue eyes. Many people said Angela inherited her eyes, before they knew both kids were adopted. She was soft spoken, with a great sense of humor and an affinity for football. Henry adored her and she was completely enamored of him. They got along better than most married couples, especially for being married for so long.

They never seemed to tire of each other. They had a lot in common so they enjoyed spending time together but also had enough separate interests to keep them going when they wanted or had to be apart.

As he exhaled, Cheryl stepped out onto the deck and slipped her arms around his waist, hugging him from behind. He smiled contentedly, reaching around and patting her softly on her rump.

Cheryl giggled, leaning her face against the warmth of his back.

"I know it's only been a couple of days but it's been great having you around all the time, hon."

Henry sighed.

"I know. I've loved every minute of it so far. You know, we should take a trip this summer with the girls. What do you think?"

"I think that's the best idea I've heard today. Where are you thinking of going?"

"Why not Up North? You know my dad's got that house in Gaylord. The girls have never been there. I think they'd love it."

"That's a great idea. When they get up, let's talk to them about it."

Henry glanced at his watch. It was nine o'clock. Since

school let out five days ago, the girls had slept in every morning for as long as they possibly could. He calculated they'd be up and running full steam within the hour. They had too much energy between them to sleep much longer. Just then a little face appeared at the sliding glass door to the kitchen, a mop of tangled red hair catching the morning sun. Angela grinned as Henry opened the door and scooped her up into his arms. Two seconds later, Nicki zombie-walked out onto the deck, rubbing her eyes to keep the sun from blinding her. Cheryl wrapped her arm around her and they all walked back into the kitchen to fix breakfast.

Over cold cereal and Henry's favorite vice, custard donuts, they discussed plans for their trip up north. The girls were ecstatic, squealing in excitement and spewing milk all over the table. They planned to go at the end of August, as Cheryl couldn't get time off work any sooner. In the meantime, Henry even volunteered to take the girls shopping for anything they might need. Cheryl, arching an eyebrow at him, wished him luck and took him up on the offer.

By the end of July, Henry had a constant headache. He was continuously popping aspirin to keep it in check but it never left him completely. He figured his body was suffering withdrawal from being out of work for a month and a half. It didn't help that his car had been in the shop for the last couple of weeks. Cheryl needed their other vehicle for work so he was stuck in the house day after day with no relief.

A week before they were to leave on vacation, Henry took the girls to the mall. He'd been feeling a bit edgy that morning and he thought a nice distracting afternoon of shopping would help him feel better. He wasn't prepared for the catastrophe that was to come.

He had no idea how often little girls had to go to the bathroom. He didn't know how loud they could get until they were refused something they wanted desperately. They tired easily and had to inspect every inch of every shiny bauble that caught their eye, which was about every 10 feet. He learned that next time he went shopping with them, he wouldn't take them into the Hallmark store and let them anywhere near the china figurines, two of which he had to pay for after Angela knocked into a shelf and broke them.

By the time they came home, the girls were exhausted and Henry was fuming. He vowed never to do that again, even if his life depended on it. As he put the shopping bags up on the kitchen table, the girls started whining about dinner. He rubbed his temples, hoping that would drown out their high-pitched nasally complaints but it only seemed to amplify them. They started tugging on his slacks, begging to have pizza, then hamburgers, then back to pizza again.

He spun around on them so quickly that Nicki never had the chance to let go of his pant leg and almost went flying to the floor. She stumbled into him and banged her knee on his shin. Her eyes started to well up but before she had a chance to even open her mouth to sob in pain, Henry screamed.

"God dammit! Will you two be quiet?"

He balled his hands into fists and shook them over the two girls. They stood in stunned silence. They'd never heard him swear before and they didn't know how to react. Nicki silently rubbed her knee and Angela hid behind her. Tears rolled down Nicki's cheeks and her bottom lip pooched out, but she was trying not to cry aloud. Angela's blue eyes looked like ice as she trembled in quiet fear.

Henry took a menacing step towards them just as

Cheryl walked through the door. She arched her eyebrow at the trio.

"So, how'd it go?" she asked.

The girls broke free from their frightened paralysis and ran to Cheryl. They clung to her legs as if they were the last remnants from a sinking ship and would save them from drowning. Nicki buried her face into the folds of Cheryl's shirt but Angela kept a wary eye on Henry from behind Cheryl's hip, as if she didn't know who he was or what he was doing in their house.

Cheryl frowned and looked up at Henry. He looked ashamed and embarrassed but there was a glint of anger behind his grey eyes. His shoulders were slumped, most likely because he felt bad, but it appeared as if he was crouching, like an animal ready to pounce on wounded prey. She led the girls away from him and up to their room, where she quieted them down and promised to order pizza for dinner.

When she came back down, Henry was sitting in the recliner in front of the TV, his head in his hands. She knelt in front of him, smoothing back his hair.

"What happened?"

"Oh, I don't know. I didn't think it would be so exhausting, you know? By the time we got home I was ready to scream. Then Nicki banged into me and I lost it."

"I probably should have prepared you for this. Even I get that way when I take them shopping. It's hard to control and keep up with two little girls. Believe me, I do know. But the trick is to remember they are just little kids. They can't help but be exhausting to adults. So don't worry, okay?"

He leaned forward and rested his head on her shoulder. She wrapped her arms around him and calmed him down, just like she did the girls. When he looked up, Nicki and

Angela were standing behind Cheryl, looking nervous. When he smiled at them, Nicki grinned and ran into his arms. He apologized for his outburst and kissed her bruised knee. He released her and turned to Angela, who stood off to the side, chewing on her bottom lip. He opened his arms to her and she slowly walked into his embrace. He hugged her gently, apologizing softly, but she stood limp and unresponsive in his arms.

He cleared his throat, gently pushing her back towards Cheryl, and changed the subject.

"Okay. Who wants pizza?"

Both girls screeched in delight and ran to the phone, their little feet pounding across the vinyl floor in the kitchen. Cheryl raced after them, grabbed the phone before they managed to break it, and held it up out of their reach as they jumped up and down, trying to grab it. Henry rubbed his temples again as they all laughed and squealed in delight at this game. He walked over to Cheryl, who stopped laughing as he loomed over her, and snatched the phone from her hand. She guided the girls outside to the backyard and frowned over her shoulder at Henry.

He punched a number into the phone and barked his order to the poor kid on the other end. When he finished, he slammed the phone down on the cradle and stood at the glass door, overlooking the deck and backyard. Cheryl and the girls were running around, playing tag, enjoying the warm August evening. Henry folded his arms across his chest and glowered at them.

Their trip up north came and went quickly. For the most part, Henry sat on the porch or in front of the TV the whole time while Cheryl and the girls took advantage of the fresh air and explored the forest behind his dad's house. The only time he took an interest in anything was when

Cheryl found a dead deer in the forest, about 20 feet from the house. He stood over the carcass, which had been half chewed by the resident scavengers, after Cheryl dragged him out to see it.

He grabbed a long thick branch from the forest floor and poked the corpse.

It was still pretty solid, where it hadn't been eaten, so he poked harder. He kept pushing at it, harder and harder, until finally, lifting his arms above his head, he rammed the stick through the ribcage. The bones snapped and cracked and gave way to the branch. He let go and it remained vertical, supported by the dead flesh and bones. Henry grinned.

He grabbed the end sticking up and pushed it around and around, grinding the opening he made in the carrion wider and wider. He looked over at Cheryl, smiling like a kid in a candy store. She backed away from him, her lip curled up in an angry snarl, her eyes clouded with disgust. She stormed off, back to the house, and Henry just stood over the dead animal, grinning.

When they returned home, Henry went straight for the basement, where he had built a home office several years ago, and locked himself in. That left Cheryl alone to struggle with the bags and the two girls, who decided they'd rather whine and complain about the vacation being over than help out. By threatening to cut off their TV privileges, Cheryl convinced the girls to bring in the cooler and the bag of dirty laundry.

As Cheryl and the girls put away their vacation things, Henry tested the lock on the office door, making sure no one could come in and disturb him. He had a desk and computer in the back right corner and a couch and TV to the left. There was even a half bath directly to the left of the door. He lifted up one of the seat cushions on the couch and pulled out a rolled up plastic bag. He opened it and took a deep whiff.

"Thank God for Carl," Henry whispered.

Carl, his best friend since high school, lived a couple of miles away and grew his own marijuana. He had a great set-up in his basement, fluorescent lights and all, and kept Henry well supplied throughout the year. He wasn't a druggie by any means but it was a nice way to unwind from a long day's work or just to relax if he was feeling a bit tense. Granted, he didn't have a job now but he seemed more stressed and agitated since he'd been spending all this time at home.

Shrugging his shoulders, he went to the bottom drawer of his desk and pulled out a blue glass bong that he'd made his Senior year of high school. He filled the bottom with water from the sink in the bathroom and packed the bowl, making sure to discard the shake. He pulled a worn gold Zippo from the top drawer of the desk and sat down on the couch.

Flicking open the lighter, he lit the weed and filled the bong with smoke. He slowly inhaled a mouthful of it, pursing his lips to keep it from seeping out too soon. Exhaling, he grinned around the smoke.

"Now that's good ganja."

He took a few more hits, starting to feel the mellowing effects of the drug. His legs and arms always went to jelly first and he flailed them around now, thinking he looked like a giant turtle stuck on its back. He giggled.

"Yeah, a turtle with a bong, man."

He lit the bowl again and filled the bong completely with smoke. He looked around, grinning, and shouted to no one in particular.

"SHOTGUN!"

He sucked all the smoke directly into his lungs, burning the back of his throat, but he managed to keep it all in for 10 seconds. His tongue tasted a bit like ashes after that but as he exhaled, he whooped loudly, sticking his index finger in the air and chanting "I'm Number On" over and over.

A loud banging sounded at the door and he looked at the computer, confused. When Cheryl called from the other side, he chuckled. He put the bong down next to the computer, asking it to keep an eye on his Mary Jane, and opened the office door. A wall of sweet smelling smoke hit Cheryl in the face and she waved it away angrily.

"Do you have to do that when the kids are home?"

Henry thought about it for a minute. As he was considering his answer, Cheryl huffed and moved into the office, closing the door behind her.

"Oh, for God's sake, Henry. What is the matter with you? You barely talk to me anymore and when you do, it's just to bitch or insult me. And the girls. Did you know they're scared of you, Henry? Nicki just tries to ignore you but Angie is terrified. She's not sleeping well and she's having nightmares. Nightmares about you, Henry. Henry? Are you even listening to me?"

Henry stood swaying slightly in front of her, a scowl darkening his features.

He caught vague glimpses through his mind of all the fighting and crying of the past few months. Cheryl did nothing but nag him these days and those girls, those little brats did nothing but whine and cry all day long. Nothing was ever good enough. All these damn females surrounding him were wearing him down. They'd beat and tear at him until there was nothing left to call a man.

He looked at the woman he had called his wife, his

soulmate, his beloved for the last 20 years. His vision clouded over with red, as if his brain had exploded behind his eyes and all he could see was blood. He reached behind her and pushed open the door. When she looked up at him, frowning, he placed his hand on her chest and shoved her out into the basement. She fell sideways and cracked her right knee against the concrete floor.

"Henry, what the hell..."

He strode over to her and grabbed her by the hair, yanking her to her feet. Her neck popped loudly as he wrenched her head back to look up at him. His eyes were cold and dark with the promise of true pain. He pulled her face close to his and he moved as if he was going to kiss her. Instead, he bit deeply into her bottom lip. He chewed on the tender flesh for a moment, flesh he had once kissed in friendship and love, and then clamped his teeth together and pulled. She screamed as blood flowed down her chin. She stared at him wide-eyed, her fingers fumbling around the raw oozing wound that was once her lower lip.

His high completely gone now and replaced with insane fury, he growled. "You know, Cheryl, you're such a kill-buzz."

He grabbed her head on both sides and placed his thumbs over her eyes.

Pushing down, he was surprised as how little pressure he needed to exert to pop her eyeballs. As the vitreous humor oozed over the backs of his hands, Cheryl howled in agony. He tipped his own head back and howled along with her, baying like a wolf at the full moon. Her knees buckled and she started to sink to the floor. Looking down at her, Henry tilted his head to the side, studying her.

"You know, Cheryl, your head would make an excellent bowling ball. Hang on a minute."

He pulled his thumbs from her eye sockets and she crumpled to the floor.

As he searched the basement for the proper tool, she tried to crawl towards the steps leading upstairs. Her hand grazed the bottom step just as Henry grabbed her ankle and dragged her backwards. She whimpered softly, not wanting the girls to hear what was happening. But if she didn't warn them somehow, they might suffer the same fate.

Before she even had a chance to think of how to warn the girls, Henry bent down close to her face, holding something cold against her neck. She winced as he pressed the teeth of the blade into her skin. The bow saw gleamed under the fluorescent lighting of the basement. Henry's eyes mirrored its sheen.

"Now, you're going to feel a slight pressure, Cheryl. But once that passes, it's gonna hurt like hell."

Cheryl opened her mouth to scream but Henry whipped the saw across her windpipe, silencing her warning cry. Blood squirted out from her neck and open mouth, spattering Henry's face and pooling onto the basement floor. She choked and gurgled on her own fluids, her arms flailing around weakly, trying to grab for Henry, who was dodging her grasp only after slapping at her reaching hands. Her arms went limp but she was still conscious, trying to suck air in through the ragged opening in her neck. Whistling, Henry knelt beside her and placed the bow saw in the open wound, causing Cheryl to arch her back in pain.

"Honey, if you don't sit still, this won't look right."

A sob whistled through her torn windpipe, the last sound she would ever make. He swung his arm back and forth, ripping through her flesh with ease, but the blade caught when he reached her backbone. He yanked the blade backwards several times before it came flying out. Pushing her head back, he looked for a space between the vertebrae where he could cut more easily. He felt a sliver of cartilage between two bones and ran the saw through there.

Cheryl's head rolled off to the right. He picked it up by the hair, turning it left and right. He walked back to his office and into the small bathroom. He rummaged through the shelf below the sink and finally found what he was looking for—the electric shaver. Propping the head up in the sink, he plugged it in and turned it on.

It only took about five minutes to shave the entire head. He held it up, sticking his fingers in the eye sockets and hooking his thumb under the front teeth. He posed for the mirror, stretching out his left arm in front of him and the right, with the head, straight out behind, as if he were about the throw the perfect strike. Laughing, he kissed the head, smearing his mouth with blood, and walked over to his desk and propped it up on top of his computer.

"Now, for those two little monsters."

Searching the basement for the appropriate weapon, he came across a portable nail gun. The compressed air cartridge only lasted long enough to shoot out 20-30 nails, but that should be enough to slow the little rats down. He wanted them alive–for now.

He checked the gun to make sure it was loaded with nails and headed up the stairs. As he entered the kitchen, he could hear the TV in the living room. A few seconds later, Nicki's tinkling laughter floated over to him and he cringed. To him it sounded like a metal rake scraping across a blackboard. He tiptoed down the hall and peeked around the corner. Nicki was sprawled on her stomach a few feet away from the television, her back to Henry. He wondered why Angela wasn't with her.

As he was deciding where to shoot her, he heard a soft creak on the staircase behind him. He slowly turned and saw a doe-eyed Angie staring at him from behind the handrail. She didn't shout or cry. She didn't ask any "why" questions. But when he took a step towards her she turned and sprinted back upstairs.

"Shit!" he yelled. That got Nicki's attention and she ran into the hallway to see what was going on. She pointed to the nail gun in his hand.

"Daddy, what's that, and why–?"

Henry spun around and pulled the trigger twice. One nail nicked her right ear and the second sailed through her open mouth, piercing the back of her throat. She collapsed to the floor, gagging on the nail and choking on blood. She seemed immobilized but just in case, he walked up to her and shot another nail into her stomach. She screamed and blood shot out her mouth, staining her white tank top and shorts.

Satisfied she wasn't going anywhere, Henry turned and ran up the stairs.

There were three bedrooms and one bathroom upstairs. He went to the girls' rooms first. Crashing through the door, he bellowed like a charging bear. Angie had spilled marbles all across the hardwood floor and Henry went down, face first, landing on top of the nail gun. The chunky metal cut into his forehead and scraped the bone.

Growling in anger, he stood slowly, tentatively touching the wound. He winced as he brushed a finger across a hanging flap of skin. He could also feel the exposed bone of his skull, slippery and smooth. His lip curled up in a snarl as he looked around the room. As he was about to look under the bed he heard a door slam out in the hall.

He rushed out of the girls' room in time to see a fiery-red blur, Angie's hair, fly towards the staircase. When he got to the top step, Angie was already halfway down, gripping the handrail to keep from falling. Henry aimed the gun and, with a lucky shot, nailed her left hand to the railing. Angie's legs shot out from beneath her when she could no longer run beyond the reach of her nailed limb. She landed on her backside with her left arm stretched above her head.

Grinning, Henry slowly walked down the steps to her. He bent down, tracing a finger across her face and up her left arm, leaving a trail of blood on her pale skin. She kept silent but watched his hand with her eyes. He gripped her left wrist and pulled, tearing her hand almost in half when he yanked it off the nail. She still did not make a sound but squeezed her eyes shut as tears spilled down her cheeks.

He frowned. Why wasn't she screaming in pain? She wasn't even whimpering, for God's sake. He shook her roughly, causing her head to bang loudly on the railing but still nothing escaped her lips. He dug his thumb into her torn hand, grinding his nail into her raw flesh but she never made a sound. Snarling, he dragged her down the last few steps and over to her sister, who was still writhing in agony on the living room floor.

Angie was struggling in his grip until her eyes fell on Nicki. Watching her sister clutch at her throat, gurgling sobs of pain bubbling out of her mouth, Angie mewled like a lost kitten. She stretched out her bleeding hand to Nicki, who was unaware her little sister was standing over her, and started crying hysterically. Henry yanked on Angie's arm and pulled her close.

"So, this is what gets a reaction out of you, huh? Oh, you're such a big man when it comes to your own pain. But when Nicki suffers..."

He pointed the nail gun at his eldest daughter and shot

three nails into her leg. Her hands flew from her throat to her right thigh, gripping at the metal protruding from the muscle. She tried to pull them out but the effort only caused her more pain and she flopped back, defeated. She saw Angie for the first time and reached out to her. Angie tugged and pulled, trying to release herself from her father's grip, but Henry only squeezed tighter. Nicki slowly lowered her hand but her eyes never left her sister's face. As the last spark of life seeped out of her, Nicki smiled softly at Angie and wiggled her fingers goodbye.

As Nicki exhaled her last breath, Angie wailed. Henry was killing her faster than if he took a ball-peen hammer to the back of her skull. Seeing as rendering emotional pain on the youngest of his brood was much more satisfying than physical torture, Henry decided it was time for Angie to see his new bowling ball. Yanking her towards the basement steps, she lost her footing and fell to her knees. She had fallen silent again but as Henry dragged her along the floor towards the basement steps, she arched her back to look over at her dead sister.

When he reached the door leading to the basement, Henry turned around, grabbed Angie's ankles, and walked down the steps backwards so he could watch her body bounce over each one. As her body passed through the open door, Angie suddenly reached for the doorjamb and clung tightly. That quick movement caused Henry to lose his footing. He let go of Angie to try and stop his backward momentum but it was too late. He tumbled and crashed down the concrete steps, cracking bones and bruising flesh, until he came to an abrupt and final stop at the foot of the stairs.

Groaning, he rolled his head to the right and screamed as pain shot down his neck. He couldn't move his legs. He must have broken his back on the way down. As he tried to move his arms white hot pain exploded on each side of him.

He looked to the right. Even though he was still holding the nail gun, his humerus was poking through the ripped cotton of his t-shirt, a small swatch of the white fabric hanging limply on the jagged end of bone. To his left, his arm looked fine but the bulge at the shoulder indicated an obvious dislocated joint.

He was truly fucked. He looked up at the ceiling and started to laugh. Each chuckle sent spasms of pain through his upper body but he couldn't stop. What a perfect ending to his rampage. He could just hear the news report: "Local man butchers family and cripples himself in a fall. Coroner determined he lived for hours, possibly days, before his corpse was discovered by police after neighbors complained about a foul stench coming from the man's home."

He sucked in a long breath and guffawed with delight. As tears rolled down his cheeks into his ears, he heard a soft sound above him. Lifting his head and grimacing at the pain, he looked up and saw Angie standing on the steps above him. She was holding her injured left hand in her right, her face like stone framed by her flaming red hair. Henry's laughter died down to soft giggles.

"Holy shit. I forgot all about you, munchkin. Hey, wanna do daddy a favor? Can you go upstairs and call '911'?"

Angie stood stoically over him, her ice blue eyes blinking once. Still grinning, Henry tried again.

"Hey, stupid, I'm talking to you. Get upstairs and call an ambulance!"

She didn't move. She only stood there, staring at him, cradling her ruined hand. Henry's mirth left him completely and he growled at her.

"God dammit, you worthless brat. Get your ass upstairs right now and do as I say or you'll really be sorry!"

Angie blinked at him in response. Henry screamed.

"What the hell is the matter with you? What do I have to do to get you to move?"

Her eyes flashed briefly with dark hatred before she whispered her answer. "Die."

Sometime in the hushed hour before dawn, a tiny figure stepped out of her front door. She looked up and down the street, holding her left hand to her chest. Her fiery red hair waved in the soft breeze as she made her way down the sidewalk to the neighbor's house and rang the bell.

"So, Luke. What's on your mind this week?" "I'm having doubts again, doc."

The therapist, Dr. Ophan, clicked his pen and began to take notes of this weekly session.

"Doubts about what?" he asked.

Luke sighed. "Oh, nothing. And everything. You know, when I first branched out on my own, it was so exciting. I could be my own boss, set my own rules. I could even break them, too. But now," he trailed off.

"But what, Luke?" Dr. Ophan prompted him to continue.

"I don't know. Everyone looks to me for everything now. I have to make all the decisions, deal with insubordinates, delegate responsibilities. It's exhausting."

"And you're wondering if you're capable of running the show."

"I guess that's it," Luke mused. "I just don't have the confidence in my own abilities anymore. Not like I used to. Maybe I shouldn't have quit. Maybe I was too rash."

"You don't really believe that do you?" the doctor asked. "That you're incapable of leadership? That you're weak?"

Luke sat up on the couch. "I never said I felt weak."

"But that's what you're alluding to, isn't it? You're not strong enough to be in charge. That you're better off taking orders instead of giving them, right?"

Luke knew his therapist was baiting him, getting him to stand up for himself, to defend his life choices. And it was working.

"What was I supposed to do? Just sit back and let it happen?"

"Well, that was your job, wasn't it? You built a very comfortable existence following management directives before. Why was this so different?"

"Because it was wrong. It was humiliating and I couldn't allow it to continue."

Dr. Ophan nodded. "This wasn't the first time, though, was it? You'd been making a stink for quite a while."

"This was different," Luke said as he shook his head in disagreement. "Sure, I made my complaints known before. I followed procedure, turned in my suggestions. When they were all ignored I went back to business as usual. But this time... I don't know. Something inside me just snapped, and I felt like I had to do something about it."

The therapist nodded, and Luke continued.

"When I spoke up this time, however, I was given an ultimatum—either fall in line or get out. I chose to leave, of course, but he knew damn well I couldn't stay so it was hardly a fair choice."

Dr. Ophan sat back in his overstuffed chair and watched Luke as he ranted.

Occasionally he looked down at his pad of paper to scribble a note or two. Luke straightened his shoulders.

"But I didn't go alone. I took a few friends with me and I started my own organization. It was hard work, which never seemed to end, but eventually the word got out. More and more were coming over to my side and my territory grew. Do you know I have at least thirty satellite offices in every major city in the world?"

"Really?" Dr. Ophan asked. "That's quite impressive."

"I know," Luke said. "And you should see some of my smaller ops. You'd think a podunk backwater hickville would be the last place to drum up business. It's surprising how fast and easy it is to set up a successful venture in towns like that."

The therapist stared at him and Luke laughed.

"Okay, okay, doc. I get it. Nicely done."

"I have no idea to what you are referring."

"You know, telling me I'm weak, afraid. Making me go on the defensive so I can get back to where I belong."

The doctor frowned. "I'm not sure what you mean."

"See, that's why I pay you the big bucks. I'm feeling much better now."

"Really?" the therapist looked up at him. "You're not just telling me what I want to hear?"

"No, doc. I mean it," Luke answered. "Faith restored. Crisis averted. Thanks."

Dr. Ophan nodded. "Anytime. Was there anything else on your mind?"

Luke shook his head. "No, I think that's enough for this week. Thanks again. I'll see you next Tuesday."

"Of course. Take care of yourself, Luke."

Dr. Ophan walked Luke to the door and escorted him out of his office. As he strolled down the corridor, Luke felt lighter, as if a great burden had been released from his shoulders and he couldn't wait to get back to work.

Luke pushed open the double doors at the end of the hallway and inhaled the sulfur fumes deep into his lungs. The screams of all the tortured souls occupying Hell tickled his inner ears and he laughed. His black skin reflected the orange and red fires like a mirror. He'd always loved having such dark flesh—the same color as volcanic glass, bubbling tar, or charred wood. Some of his favorite things.

He strolled down one of the corridors that led to his office in the center.

Steel doors dotted each side of the hallway and Luke could hear various grunts and wails coming from the rooms behind each one. He popped his head into the closest room on his left.

Gressil, one of the great masters of pain in Hell, worked over a pale thin man strapped to a large spinning iron wheel. The man was naked, and most of his skin had been flayed off by the sharp scalpel in Gressil's hand. Luke waved as the demon paused his work.

"Sorry, don't stop on my account. Just wanted to see how things were going."

"Everything's great. Allow me to introduce Malcolm. Malcolm, this is Luke. He runs the joint."

Malcolm gaped but managed to sputter out one word.

"Lucifer?"

Luke smiled.

"I prefer Luke. But Lucifer, Satan, Apollyon, Prince of Darkness, whatever works. Although I don't much care for Beelzebub. I never really got that one."

Gressil shook his head. "Yeah, me neither."

"So, what's Malcolm in for?"

"Pedophile," Gressil grinned, his razor sharp teeth, packed in his mouth in rows like a great white shark, glinted in the flames from the wall sconces. He held the scalpel out to Luke.

"Would you care to give it a go?"

"What? And ruin the great work you've done so far? I wouldn't dream of it."

Gressil smiled again as he picked up a long thin strip of skin from the floor at Malcolm's feet.

"This is probably some of my best work, if I do say so myself. Perhaps tomorrow, sir?"

Luke grinned. "Perhaps. Please continue." He smiled at the thin man. "Nice meeting you, Malcolm. Enjoy your eternity."

He closed the door and smiled when Malcolm's cries echoed into the hall. Three doors further down, Luke overheard a demon arguing with a damned soul.

"Please, miss. If you could just move over there."

"Are you fucking crazy? I'm not doing anything of the sort. Do you know who I am? Do you have any idea the kind of fuck up that's happened here? I'll have my attorney on your ass so fast it'll make your head spin."

Luke knocked on the door then eased it open a few inches. "Hello? Mind if I interrupt?"

The demon, Agrat, smiled with relief when she saw him. "Lord Lucifer, by all means, please come in."

He walked over to her and gave her a peck on the cheek. "And how's my favorite demoness today?"

Agrat looked over at her assigned soul and shook her head.

"Not so good, sir. It seems Miss Morse here," she began before the woman interrupted her.

"That's miz to the likes of you, bitch."

"Miz Morse seems to think there's been a mix up."

Luke frowned.

"What kind of mix up?"

"She believes she was sent to the wrong location, sir."

He nodded. "Ah, I understand. Do you have Miss, excuse me, Miz Morse's file handy?"

Agrat grabbed it from the nearby table and handed it to Luke. He hefted the thick folder in his hand.

"Whoa, kinda heavy, isn't it?" he remarked as he winked at the woman. "All right, let's see here. Extortion, bribery, kidnapping, prostitution, drug trafficking, matricide, destruction of property, sleeping your way through grad school, cheating on your junior year geography exam, and stealing Josie Fillian's lunch money every day in fifth grade. Well, Miz Morse, you are absolutely correct. You do not belong here."

The woman crossed her arms over her chest and sneered at Agrat. "You see, little bitch? I told you."

Agrat looked at Lucifer, stunned and confused. He snapped the folder closed and handed it back to her.

"Yes, this thing never should have come to your office, Agrat. I'm so sorry about the mix up. Her kind is reserved for Level Four Hundred and Thirty Two. I'll have her transferred to Malphas' department immediately."

The demon smiled, her forked tongue licking her razor thin lips, and bowed to Luke. "Thank you so much, sir. I knew I should have said something when Nybras brought her here."

"Nybras? What in my name was he doing transporting a soul?"

Agrat shrugged. "Maybe he was bored?"

"Huh. Well, if he spent more time on the newsletter, like he's supposed to, we'd have more comprehensible issues and fewer spelling errors. I'll talk to him. In the meantime..."

Luke turned to Miz Morse, flicking a finger in her direction. A pair of thick steel shackles enveloped her wrists. Before she could squeak out a response, he conjured another pair for her ankles. With a third movement, he secured the shackles to the wall, leaving the woman to hang, thrashing in anger.

"What is this? I demand to see the manager!"

In a flash he crushed his body against hers, their noses touching. He breathed sulfur into her open mouth.

"I am the manager. I am the manager, the director, the social chair, the caretaker, the boss. I am Legion."

The woman gulped down her fear the best she could and stuttered a reply. "B-b-but I don't belong here."

"Liar, liar, pants on fire," Luke sang with a youthful lilt. The woman blinked.

"That's a bit childish, isn't it?"

"No, really. You're pants are on fire."

Miz Morse looked down to see her legs aflame. She screamed as the fire seared into her flesh. Her cheap suit bubbled as it melted from the heat.

"Ooooh, polyester. Bad choice."

Agrat raised her hand to give Luke a high five. "Good one, sir."

"That'll keep her busy until we can get her transferred. I'll send Kobal down here and get this all straightened out. Better?"

"Yes, thank you."

"Next time don't you feel squeamish about speaking up, all right?"

Agrat nodded. "I won't."

"That's my girl."

Luke left Agrat's office and shut the door on Miz Morse's shrieks. As he made his way closer to his office,

Kobal, one of the many imps that assisted Luke, came running toward him. Even from here Luke could hear the imp's labored breathing. Kobal seemed to have his little shiny gold pants in a bunch about something.

"My Lord, I need your help. I can't figure out who should take care of these souls."

He handed three files to Luke, who sighed when he took them, then perused their contents. As he read, Luke continued walking and the imp had to jog to keep up.

"All right. Let's put Carreau on the murderer, and assign Asmoday to the little lady who slept with every man in the northern hemisphere besides her husband. Sheesh, she really got around, didn't she? And this last one—whoa."

Luke stopped walking. He pulled out the photo from the third file and turned it sideways. He spoke to Kobal but never took his eyes off the picture.

"Is this guy doing what I think he's doing?"

The imp nodded.

"Yes, sir."

"With a pig?"

"Uh huh."

Luke held the picture closer to study the details.

"And those?"

"Midgets? Yes, sir."

"And they're...?"

"Yep."

"With?"

"Snakes and honey, yes, sir."

Luke laughed then handed the other two files back to Kobal. "Bring him to me. I've got to meet this guy."

"As you wish, my Lord."

"Oh, and get a clerk over to Agrat's office for a soul transfer. And tell Nybras I want to see him ASAP."

He watched the imp as he ran off down the hall, then disappeared behind the last door on the right. Luke smiled as he turned back to walk to his office. A large black goat trotted down the hall toward him. Luke nodded at it.

"Hello, Leonard."

The goat bleated at him and continued on its way.

"Man I love my job," Luke said aloud to himself. "Imagine, I doubted the wisdom of all this. What was I thinking?"

Luke whistled as he reached his office door.

After bidding Luke farewell, Dr. Ophan closed his office door. He sat down in a leather burgundy desk chair then picked up a small tape recorder. Clicking the record button, he cleared his throat before speaking.

"Ah, Tuesday, March fifth. Session number 133,216,148. Subject: Luke Prince. Subject experienced his annual breakdown in regards to quitting management. Said breakdown occurs every year on the anniversary of his resignation. Subject is confronted with issues of self-doubt and loathing, questioning his abilities as a leader and effectiveness therein. I applied successful technique of catering to his massive ego by confirming aforementioned doubts and belittling his concerns. Anticipate that subject will be emotionally stable until the next anniversary. Side note: Management should be pleased with today's session results."

MOTHER KNOWS BEST

The dark rectangle of the open door squatted in the middle of the dirty white wall. Old and faded paint flakes fell from the crumbling bricks and scattered across the cracked blacktop. The low breeze picked up bits of trash and debris and tossed them in the air. A discarded coffee cup rolled around the empty lot surrounding the low hulking building.

The structure seemed benign, but Robert knew what lay beyond. He stood before the doorway, afraid to move forward but never considering the idea of turning back. What awaited him inside was not as horrible as what would befall him if he didn't go in. That black opening was the gateway to Hell, but it was preferable to defying her.

Beyond the door lay pain, humiliation, and death. He could almost smell the fresh blood and feces of their latest 'volunteer'. Was that a whimper? No, impossible. The man was strapped to a metal gurney deep in the bowels of the abandoned hospital. No one could hear him scream, let alone any soft cries, from up here. Maybe Robert was simply hearing his own desperate panicked breaths.

His cell phone chirped from inside his coat pocket. He flipped it open and spoke, hoping it was a wrong number.

"Hello?"

"Robert? What's taking you so long? I can't finish the cleansing until you bring the supplies. Where are you?"

"I'm here, Mother. I'll be down in a moment."

"Make it snappy. He's fading fast. There isn't much time."

"Of course."

Robert snapped the phone closed and placed it back in his pocket. He bent down and picked up several canvas bags, the kind grocery stores sold to help you 'go green'. The jugs of hydrochloric acid were heavy and he struggled with them until he distributed the weight evenly between his hands.

The wind kicked up and lifted the few grey strands of hair he combed over the top of his balding pate. He took a deep breath then stepped into the darkness.

S he traced her fingers along the surface of the water. The mini waves she created threatened to spill over the edges of the tub and onto her mother's precious blue tiles. How many times had Angie lay on these tiles pressing a newly bruised cheek against their cool surfaces? How many times had she curled up around the toilet careful not to vomit the spoiled food her mother had forced her to eat onto their sapphire beauty?

Angie flicked her finger against the water and watched as several drops flew outward and splashed to the floor. Smiling, she did it again. Small puddles gathered on the tiles around her. She splashed and laughed until her dress was soaked through and the tiles, including the pristine grout, lay under a shallow sheet of bathwater.

It wasn't as hard as she thought it'd be. A quick swing of her piano trophy, a simple push, and it was over. Angie stared at her mother's body in the water and the frozen look of surprise on her face. A thin line of blood trailed from her mother's head to the surface.

She reached down through the water and twirled a lock

of her mother's hair around her finger. After tugging it several times and seeing no reaction, Angie grabbed a fistful and yanked it back and forth. More water splashed to the floor but her mother never flinched.

Good.

Leaving her in the bathroom, Angie walked down the hall. She left wet footprints behind but she no longer had to worry about the consequences. Once in her own room, she moved to the portable radio on her dresser and unplugged it from the wall. It was the last gift her father ever gave her.

Angie felt tears roll down her cheeks as she went back to the bathroom. If her father hadn't left, if he hadn't found a new family to love, Angie's mother never would have...

Well, it didn't matter now. When she returned to the bathroom, Angie plugged the radio into the wall socket next to the sink. Standing next to the tub, she stared down at the submerged form of her mother. Angie sighed then placed the radio on the floor.

She reached down and pulled her mother's body up and propped it against the faucet. Angie stepped into the tub, slowly lowering herself until she was waist deep in the water. Some sloshed over the side and joined the other puddles on the floor.

"Mother, I'm sorry," Angie muttered, so accustomed to feeling shame and fear for every mistake she ever made. She reached over and picked up the radio, flipped the 'on' switch, and held it above the water. Before she knew it, Angie had snuggled up against her mother's corpse, almost as if trying to find one last comfort in a mother she had never known.

"Maybe we'll get it right in the next life," Angie whispered before she dropped the radio into the water.

FESTER

Joe stood teetering on the small stepladder as he tried to re-hang the antique cuckoo clock in the kitchen. The ornate piece, something he always considered tacky and gaudy, was passed down to his wife from her great Aunt Gretchen as a wedding gift. Like most of the other knick-knacks and tchotchkes they inherited from her side of the family, the clock was just another example of 1950's kitsch that made their entire house look like a reject from the Wisconsin Dells; completely hokey, and just enough smarm to fool the tourists into thinking it was quaint instead of utterly ridiculous.

The problem with the clock was that the hook on the back was extremely small and almost fully flushed with the backing. It made a very difficult and frustrating job of hooking it over the nail in the wall. By the seventh failed attempt at hanging it, and the fifth time of poking himself in the eye with the corner leaf design, Joe was ready to throw the damn clock through the kitchen window.

Blowing roughly through his teeth and lowering the clock down to give his arms a rest, he turned to look at his wife. Eileen's back was to him, and her perfectly coifed bottle-blonde hair stood motionless. Joe couldn't figure out how she did it but once her hair was styled, it never moved—at all. Did she use an entire bottle of hair spray? Was shellac mixed in? He could pour a gallon of boiling water over her head and it would all just roll off in perfectly rounded beads and splatter at her feet.

Her hair hadn't changed from the day they were married thirty years ago.

Unfortunately, her ass and her personality had switched places. She'd always been outgoing and boisterous in her younger days, with a tiny little figure. Now her backside could block out the sun and her disposition had soured and shriveled like a grape left on the vine past its prime.

Her head bobbed up and down as she chewed down another mouthful of truffles. She was staring out the window over the sink into the backyard. Joe couldn't even begin to imagine why she stood there for what seemed like hours at a time. Maybe she was looking for her lost youth—or maybe just her size four pants.

She reached back to scratch her ass and knocked over her glass of chocolate milk. It sailed to the floor and shattered all over the burnt orange and avocado green mushroom-patterned linoleum tile. She lazily looked down at the mess and slowly raised her eyes to Joe, who still stood on the rickety stepladder.

He looked from her to the broken glass to the clock cradled in his arms and back to her. She'd already turned back to the window and popped another truffle into her mouth, her lips smacking loudly around the sugary morsel. Grinding his teeth quietly, he maneuvered his way down the ladder and roughly laid the clock on the table.

"Don't you have that clock hung up yet, Joe?" Eileen barked.

"No, dear. Not yet."

"Why not?"

"Well, I..."

"Just make sure you don't break it."

"No, dear. I won't."

She glanced over her shoulder at the bits of glass on the floor.

"Aren't you going to clean that up?"

"Yes, dear. I'll take care of it."

Joe stooped over and scooped up the broken glass. Even though Eileen was the one who knocked the damn thing off the counter, the fat cow could never be bothered to clean it up herself. Mumbling oaths under his breath, as Joe would rather eat the broken glass than be confrontational, he reached for the largest piece. He promptly speared his thumb on a jagged edge and yelped. Stuffing his bleeding digit into his mouth, he stood and tossed the piece into the plastic garbage can.

Joe wiggled his lips around his thumb to snarl at this wife's back as she stood at the sink, still staring out the window into the backyard. He would never actually say anything to cause a commotion. He hated confrontation, and not just with Eileen, either. He was like that with everyone. He'd rather slice his thumb open on broken glass than have to say something negative to anyone. He liked everyone to be calm, peaceful, and happy, even if that meant he had to swallow every bad thought, like a lump of burning coal, to keep it that way. He was definitely a bottler —he stuffed all his bad feelings and emotions way down deep into his gut until they went away. If he were stressed out, he'd just clench his jaw tightly, maybe mumble a few curses, and move on.

"Goddamn lousy piece of shit glass. And that fuckin' bitch won't even..."

"What was that, Joe?"

"Oh, nothing. Just cut myself." "But what did you say?"

"What? No, nothing really. Just 'ouch'. That's all."

Mumbling some more, he walked to the bathroom for a bandage. Wrapping it around his thumb, he got back to the kitchen just as the phone rang. He picked it up.

"Hello? Oh, hello, Brian. Fine, thanks. You? Yes, your mother's good, too. How's school? What? You do? What happened to the $500 we sent you last week? Oh. Well, yes, I understand that books are expensive but...yes, food takes money, too. Yes, Brian, I'm aware of that but...Well, all right. OK. We'll wire you some tomorrow. Do you want to say hello to your moth... Brian? Hello?"

Joe gently placed the phone back in the cradle. Eileen frowned at him. "Why didn't you give me the phone so I could talk to him? You know, you're not the only parent he's got. He's my son, too, Joe."

Joe opened his mouth to reply. He wanted to tell her that their thankless spawn didn't give him a chance to pass the phone. He wanted to say that their idiot son never wanted to talk to her because all she did was compare his worthlessness to his father's, complain about the lack of excitement in her life, and ask why he wasn't more grateful to them for ponying up his college tuition so he could make something of himself unlike his useless father.

He wanted to say so many things to her but instead he grimaced and shrugged his shoulders. She raised her hands in disgust.

"Never have anything to say, do you, Joe? You can't let it

out, eh? You just stand there with your pinched face and vacant eyes, shrugging your shoulders. God, it's no wonder I don't want to have sex with you anymore."

Slowly squeezing his hands open and closed, he walked over to the remaining glass scattered on the floor. Pulling the garbage can close, he bent down and tossed the strewn shards into it, muttering to himself and flinging each piece with more fervor than the last. Finally getting all the glass off the floor, he pushed the can back into the corner. Looking down at his thumb he saw more blood dripping from the already soaked bandage.

He quickly walked back to the bathroom to get a fresh one. He stumbled over Pete, their old and fat German Shepherd, and slapped his hand against the wall to keep from falling down. He painted a bloody smear across the faded daisy wallpaper. He looked down at the dog, shaking a finger at it and wriggling his mouth with unspoken admonishments. Pete looked up at him impassively, bent down to sniff Joe's slipper sock, lifted his leg and promptly peed on him.

The dog sauntered off into the kitchen looking for a snack. Joe clenched his jaw, the muscles bulging his skin like there was an infestation of cockroaches just beneath the surface. He turned towards the bathroom when a hot searing pain ripped through his gut. He collapsed to his knees, feeling underneath his shirt for the molten-hot sword he knew must be piercing his stomach, for nothing else could have caused him so much pain.

He bent over until his forehead touched the floor. Weakly, he called out to Eileen. He could hear her, doting over that damned dog, telling him how he was such a pretty boy, such a good boy, did he want a biscuit, oh who's mommy's precious little boy? Joe tried to call out again but only managed a strangled puff of air that didn't even stir the dog hairs on the carpet. Lying down on his side, he pulled himself slowly towards the kitchen, digging his fingers into the dingy yellow shag carpet, making a sloth's pace along the hall.

Someone was now trying to pry open his skull with a hammer and chisel, and Joe gripped his head with both hands. This time he was able to scream, the pain providing the fuel for his lungs, and Eileen came running out of the kitchen. Not knowing Joe was only mere inches from the entrance to the kitchen she was unable to stop her forward momentum when she turned the corner into the hall. She kicked Joe in the face and fell forward, all 160 pounds of her landing on his upturned hip. His pelvis crunched and splintered under her weight and a new agony filled his brain. For the briefest of moments Joe knew the torment of Hell's eternal fires before falling into the blissful black pool of unconsciousness.

He woke to the soft beeping of a heart-rate monitor in St. Joseph's hospital.

The offbeat rhythm of his heart reminded him of how his grandmother used to walk-shuffle-limp with her knobby oak cane down the steps of her front porch. He never was sure if she would make it down the five steps unscathed or miss them all together and land in a crumpled heap on the sidewalk.

He looked down at the IV attached to a throbbing vein in the back of his left hand. He expected some kind of saline drip to be feeding his body like he always saw in the movies. But the IV was delivering blood to his system, not water. His initial pain-clouded thought was that he was bleeding to death from his cut finger so he raised his hand to examine the damaged digit. It was tightly wrapped in thick gauze that was sodden with blood. Eyes wide, he studied the bandages only to discover they didn't just cover his cut finger. He trailed the white fuzzy wrappings all the way up his arm and they, too, were crimson with his blood.

Confused and scared now, he turned to see his wife asleep in a chair next to the bed. Frowning, he glanced over at the wall clock that read 4:55pm. It had only been a couple of hours since he cut himself. What the hell was she doing asleep already? He supposed she couldn't be bothered to stay worried about him long enough to wait for him to wake up. God damned bitch only thought about herself. Heaven forbid if I get sick and interfere with her plans to...

His stomach lurched painfully and he belched a mouthful of blood onto his hospital gown. The heart monitor bleeped erratically as his heart skipped and stuttered. He panicked, his breathing became shallow and sped up, bringing him closer to hyperventilation. The gauze on his arm was now dripping with blood as if it was seeping right out of his pores.

He threw his arm out towards his wife for help and he cracked his hand against the bed rails. Three of this fingers snapped, the metacarpals folded inwards like the legs of a card table, and the wrist bones squished like soggy meatballs. He screamed like a banshee on fire and Eileen jumped, almost falling out of her chair. As she approached Joe's bedside, the nurse came running in from the hall. Pushing Eileen out of the way the nurse gingerly raised Joe's arm to study the damage.

She scowled at Eileen, her Jamaican accent reverberated off the crisp white walls. "What the hell did you do to him? His hand is completely destroyed."

"I didn't do anything. I was sleeping. He woke me up when he started screaming."

The nurse's scowl deepened. "You were asleep? Lady, you've only been in here for half an hour. Aren't you even worried about him? Or did all those tests he went through wear you out?"

Eileen opened her mouth to reply but the nurse held up her hand. "I don't even want to know what you have to say for yourself. Just get out of my way."

She pushed Eileen back into the chair and turned back to Joe. Another nurse came in and she ordered her to get more bandages, splints, and some morphine. Joe whimpered in pain but a soft smile curled his lips. The nurse cocked her head and couldn't help but smile back.

"What's up, hon? Why are you smiling?"

Joe shook his head, unable to respond. He just thought it was funny that a complete stranger was able to say what he never could. The nurse continued to smile at him, talking softly and soothingly as she injected the morphine into his IV. She gently splinted his fingers and slipped a plastic splint onto his wrist until they could cast it. As she finished the doctor walked in. His face twisted with grim puzzlement.

"Good afternoon, Mr. and Mrs. Smith. I had the lab put a rush on your tests so the results have come back already. I, uh....well, I don't know how to say this."

Eileen blew out an exasperated breath. "Oh, for goodness sake, doctor. You're just like Joe. Never just come out and say what you want. What is it? What's happening to him?"

The doctor flipped through a handful of papers, trying to avoid looking directly at Joe or his wife.

"Well, I'm sorry, but we just don't know what's happening. It seems his body—internal organs, bones, connective tissues, muscles—everything is breaking down. It's liquefying at an amazing speed. It looks almost like Ebola or something similar but there's no trace of any virus or bacteria. It's as if his entire body is a festering wound but there's no cause that we can find. And...and we can't do anything to stop it."

Eileen's face drooped, probably more with fear of what she'd do when Joe was dead than with worry for his suffering and pain. As Joe studied her saggy countenance, he thought about how he wished he could just tell her to go to Hell and take their sorry excuse for a son with her. A knife of pain sliced through his head and it was then that he realized what was killing him.

All these years of bottling up his emotions, all this time of biting his tongue so as not to speak any harsh or hurtful words to anyone, had finally turned on him. All those feelings didn't just go away with time. They sat in his gut, churning like a severe case of botulism, seeping disease and decay slowly out into his bloodstream, attacking his tissues with acidic precision, until the remaining globules and viscous juices could no longer be contained. He was being consumed from the inside out by repressed fear, frustration, anger, and hate.

Joe shifted in bed. He struggled to sit upright, but leaning on his un-splinted arm caused the humerus to bend like a bow saw. The bone had become soft like a wet sponge. The tissues underneath had turned to soup and that was what was seeping into the already soaked bandages. The first nurse walked around the bed, opposite of Eileen, put her arms under Joe's shoulders and lifted him up into a better sitting position. Blood and goopy bits of tissue gushed out of his body when she lifted him, slopping onto the sheets.

Moaning, Joe laid his head back on the pillow. He gripped his stomach as it churned with the pain of a hundred stabbing spikes of fired steel. It felt like he had swallowed a mace dipped in acid. His head ached, and he could feel a warm ooze flowing out of his ears. He could hear someone, possibly the doctor, arguing with the nurse on how to keep his brains from seeping out of his head. His pillow felt warm as blood trickled down his scalp and neck. He turned to look at his wife.

Eileen leaned in close, her hands vise-like on the bedrails. He worked his lips, trying to speak. His jaw creaked open, he closed his eyes in concentration, but he couldn't speak. Frustrated, he jerked his body forward as if that could force the words out of his mouth, like trying to dislodge the last bit of ketchup from the bottle by slamming the bottom of it with your hand. Eileen's face was pinched and red in anger. She screamed.

"What? Tell me. Talk to me, Joe. Just say it! Open your mouth, for Christ's sake, and spit it out!"

With one final violent lurch, Joe pitched forward and opened his mouth.

A gush of fluid sprayed onto Eileen's face. The soggy remains of his stomach, along with any bits of internal organs that hadn't liquefied, spewed forth and rolled off his wife's hair, clung to her sweater, and slushed into a puddle at her feet. With a half smile, Joe fell back against the bed. With his dying breath, he was finally able to share with her everything he'd kept inside.

REBORN

They escaped whatever it was that they had awakened in the dark. For now.

Emily stood on the front steps as she gasped for breath. When she and Ryan ran upstairs from the hidden basement, the heel broke on one of her shoes. She shambled as she clawed at the railing, the countertop in the kitchen, and the Queen Ann table in the formal dining room before bursting through the front door. Even handicapped, Emily moved faster than Ryan who didn't catch up for almost half a minute.

He clutched a handmade diary in his arms, a handful of its yellowed and brittle pages hung loose from the binding.

"Holy shit, what was that?" Ryan asked as he bent over, struggling to regain his breath and still his pounding heart.

"I think it was Carlton Rivers."

He straightened and frowned. "You can't be serious. You're talking about the original owner of Marrison Manor. The *dead* original owner."

Emily grimaced as she pressed a hand against the stitch

in her side. What the hell had they done? She was just supposed to come here, air the place out, and make sure it was ready for the open house next week. Her boss at Mainway Realty had been *very* specific with his instructions this morning.

"All you have to do is open a few windows and look the place over. If it's dirty, I'll send out a cleaning crew. If there's any structural damage, I'll call Hal and have him take care of it. Don't go poking around. I know you've heard the stories. We all have. Hell, that house is over two hundred years old. It's bound to have a little mystery surrounding it. But if the historical society thinks anything has been tampered with, and I mean so much as a thread from the cushion of a parlor chair, it's my ass in the wood chipper. You got me?"

She remembered saluting him. "Yes sir, boss man. You can count on me."

Only it turned out he couldn't. Emily did as instructed: she opened several windows upstairs and down, shook out the dust from the curtains, and noted a few places where the support beams looked a little shaky. But after she told Ryan to check the basement, she'd gone into one of the upstairs bedrooms and dug through the tiger maple bureau where she found the most beautiful cameo she'd ever seen in the top drawer.

A thin layer of grimy dust covered it. Untouched and forgotten for years, maybe decades, what harm would it do if she took it now? Emily slipped the ivory and pink carnelian shell pendant into the pocket of her suit jacket just before Ryan called to her from downstairs.

Now they both stood outside the Marrison Manor, shaking and out of breath.

"I think when we opened the door to the basement, we brought him back or let him loose or whatever."

"How is that even possible?" Ryan asked.

"I should know? You read his diary with me. It would explain the strange occurrences over the past century or so. His presence was strong enough to scare the crap out of people. Maybe he was trapped down there so he couldn't do any real harm."

Ryan's eyes widened as he remembered something. He pulled open the diary and flipped through to one of the last pages.

"What are you reading?"

"His final entry. Listen to this. 'Whatever sins Emily has committed against me...'"

Carlton shook hands with Simon one final time before imprisoning himself in the cellar. Simon begged him again to forget this foolishness, to come have a drink by the fire and talk as men. Though he appreciated the extension of camaraderie, even from a slave, Carlton could never allow himself the privilege of human companionship again.

He slammed the three heavy iron bolts into place. Simon's soft cries, muffled by the thick wooden door, could not deter him. Carlton grabbed a woolen blanket and stuffed it into the crack between the door and the cold stone floor. He could no longer hear any sounds from outside his confinement.

The small oil lamp he carried shone wan yellow light that attempted to penetrate the deep shadows of the cool room. He could just make out the edges of a low table sitting against the far wall. Carlton shuffled his way over to it, placed the lamp atop its smooth surface then collapsed into a worn wooden chair. Several sheets of parchment, an ink well and quill pen, and his pistol lay in a small circle of light. After several failed attempts to still his shaking hand, Carlton finally put pen to paper and wrote his last journal entry.

Whatever sins Emily has committed against me, they are not so great as those I have committed against her and The Almighty. My rage and self-loathing have put that harlot in the ground, and I will soon follow. I will ask Lucifer himself to rule over my damnation. I deserve nothing more than to fester in my own hatred. This land will be my prison. This house, my cell.

I will confine myself to this cellar. The slave, Simon, has given me the proper implements and text to seal this chamber, and my soul within it. Once I have performed his hoodoo ritual, I will begin my confinement at the end of a barrel.

The last thing I can hope is that all of humanity stay away from my land.

Though I fear my hate will spill onto the innocent, as long as the barrier is kept whole, I will never escape my rightful torment. May the Devil never let me go.

Carlton laid the quill on the parchment and took a deep breath. He walked to one of the dark corners where he picked up the candles, herbs, blood, and spell book that Simon had provided. After moving to the center of the cellar, he did as the slave instructed. Once the circle was drawn in blood and the correct mixture of herbs sprinkled in the four directions, Carlton went to the table and picked up his pistol.

When he stepped back inside the circle, he chanted the

spell Simon had given him then put the barrel of the gun against his temple.

"God forgive me."

He pulled the trigger.

"...may the Devil never let me go."

"Seems like his fear has come to pass, thanks to us," Emily said. "We have to get the hell out of here. My car is— oh shit!"

Ryan spun around to look back at the house.

"What? Is he coming?"

"My keys! I think I left them on the back porch. Shit!"

"Okay, okay. Crap. Um, I'll go get them. You just hide somewhere in case he comes out."

"That's your plan?"

Ryan was off and running before she could follow. She didn't want to stay out here by herself but she sure as hell didn't want to go back inside, either. So she stepped over to the towering oak tree in the front yard and huddled behind it.

Emily shivered in the October night. Over the sounds of her ragged breathing and clattering teeth, a hum echoed through the dark. It changed to a soft vibration as the ground began to tremble beneath her feet. She studied the shaking leaves of the oak tree and swallowed, her throat muscles tightening around a bitter lump of unease.

The tremors strengthened and became sound. It resembled the droning of a million insects until she picked out a rhythm within the white noise. *Thump-thump-thump-thump.* Over and over she could hear the throbbing quartet. Her skin prickled when she realized it was the hoof beats of a galloping horse.

She turned to look down the street, expecting to see a knight in shining armor rallying his trusty steed to her rescue. Only the dark and empty road laid behind her. She turned back toward the house. A plume of dust crawled out from behind it. The clopping hooves grew louder. A shimmering wave sprung up in front of the gritty cloud, like heat waves rising off a blacktop road under a clear summer sky.

Emily frowned. It couldn't be. The wavering force preceding the dust cloud darkened. Somewhere in the distance she heard someone shout her name but was too transfixed by the apparition forming before her eyes to care about its source.

The black figure sharpened further into focus. It straddled an equally black horse and was tear-assing around the corner of the manor. With each stride, the details of both horse and rider emerged, the edges becoming sharper and more defined. Emily could make out the brown leather breeches tucked into black boots. A lacy cravat bobbed up and down, its white linen a stark contrast to the crimson waistcoat and green woolen greatcoat. It was the raw gaping wound in his temple, however, that identified the dark rider as Carlton Rivers.

The aged and yellowed pages of Rivers' diary swam into her memory.

The hatred and anger he felt toward his wife, Emily, was the impetus to his self- imprisonment. She had betrayed his trust and love and he killed her for it.

Emily finally realized she and the dead man's spouse shared the same name. She didn't think hiding behind a tree was such a good idea any more. Glancing one last time at the advancing horseman, Emily turned to run. A wave of nausea crashed down on her and the sky and ground changed places. She dropped to her knees as dizziness squeezed her head like a vise. Her vision blurred at the edges and just as she thought she would black out, it released her. She shook her head and stood, using the giant oak for support.

Emily shook the dirt free from the skirt of her gown and petticoats.

Smoothing her hands over the silk stomacher, she checked to make sure nothing was torn. The stays were unbroken and still provided strong support for her back. She touched the lace cap on her head and found it askew. As she adjusted it, she felt a frown crawl across her brow.

She looked down at her clothing. A moment ago she was wearing a crisp black rayon suit, accented by black leather shoes with one broken heel. She now stood in a dark blue silk gown, a small cameo pinned at her breast, and her waist cinched in what she guessed was a corset. She looked like she had just walked out of Colonial Williamsburg.

"What the hell?"

Emily turned at the sound of approaching hoof beats. The unearthly rider slowed his shivering beast with a hard pull of the reins and a haze of dust enveloped them. Emily looked back at the manor. Ryan stood on the steps in the porch light. He frowned as he stared at her but his face fell slack with fear when he saw the sinister horseman.

She turned back to stare up at Rivers as he towered over her, his steed black as a bottomless chasm. His eyes flared with hate as he tugged on the reins to keep the horse in control. He reached into his coat and pulled out a flintlock pistol.

Cocking the hammer, he pointed the gun directly at Emily's face.

"Now, harlot, it is time to meet thy maker. Perhaps He will forgive you your sins, for I cannot."

———

Ryan ran forward as the blast echoed through the night but he was too late. Emily and Carlton Rivers faded into the darkness leaving nothing but the smell of black powder hanging in the air.

BAD TOUCHING

Rory bent over, hands on his knees, and laughed until his stomach ached. His wife, Ray, had just slipped on the muddy embankment of the slope where they had been walking and rolled into the shallow remnants of Miller's Pond. This small body of water would be at least five feet deep by summer but in early April, an inch of slimy muck, punctuated with tiny pockets of brackish water, lay in its stead. And in this gunk sat his beautiful wife.

The mud painted her peachy complexion with black smears. Her cropped golden hair lay plastered to her skull under a dripping layer of slime. Ray stared up at him as he laughed, her full lips pulled down into a tight grimace, her sky-blue eyes demanding help. As he extended his hand, Rory eased his way down to his disgruntled wife.

"You know, instead of being a douche, you could simply help me out." Rory coughed as he brought his laughter under control.

"I'm sorry, hon. Really. But you should have seen the look on your face when your feet went out from under you."

"Yes, I'm sure it was terribly amusing. Come on, help me." "You know you would've laughed if it happened to me."

He stood at the edge of the soupy muck, trying not to ruin his good hiking shoes, as he reached for Ray's outstretched hand.

"Well, it didn't happen to you. It happened to me. And now I'm cold, wet, and my ass is killing me."

A short bark of laughter flew out of his mouth before he could stifle it. She glared up at him and a glop of thick mud fell from the edge of her bangs and onto her nose, painting a dark stripe down to its tip. She stared at it, her eyes crossing, and he laughed again. When she looked up at him, her mouth twitched with a smile.

"It's not funny."

"Yes, dear."

"I'm serious. It's not funny."

This time he allowed his laughter to ring out and she joined him. He wrapped both of his hands around her left arm and pulled. She swung her right arm around and grabbed onto him. As he pulled her free from the swampy ground, Ray accidentally raked her nails across his skin, digging bloody tracks across his hand.

"Ow! Shit!"

"Oh god. I'm so sorry, Rory. Are you all right?"

When he was sure she was out of the mud, he released her and looked at his hand. The flesh rose in four angry gashes, three of them bleeding. He pulled a handkerchief from his back pocket and pressed it against the wounds.

"Let me see," Ray said.

"It's fine, hon. Don't worry."

"Just let me see, Rory."

He removed the handkerchief and Ray gasped. "Crap. Those don't look good."

"It's not that big a deal. You just scratched me. Look, it still works." Rory raised his hand and wiggled his fingers at her.

"It's not that, Rory. I don't want them to get infected. Who knows what kind of bacteria is lurking in that filth I just fell in? We gotta get you home and clean that up."

"All right, all right. Let's go, Slippy McStumbleton." Ray slapped at his arm then pushed him ahead.

The following morning, Rory awoke in a pile of sweat-soaked sheets. His stomach felt like it was full of rusted nails and though his sweaty boxers and t-shirt suggested his body temperature was high, he shivered like he was naked in the Arctic. When he groaned, Ray stirred next to him.

"Rory? What's wrong?"

"I...I don't know. I feel like hammered shit."

Ray sat up, rubbing her eyes, then looked at him. The expression on her face told him that he must look like hammered shit covered in pus swimming in vomit.

"Christ, Rory. You look awful. Let me get the thermometer. I think you have a fever."

As she hurried to the bathroom, he muttered as he scooched back under the covers.

"Gee, ya think, Einstein?"

"I heard that," she called to him.

He grumbled but said nothing more, just waited to either have his temperature taken or die, whichever came first. He almost preferred death. Ray returned from the bathroom with a slender digital thermometer. Though he usually hated to be 'mothered' by his wife, Rory didn't protest this time and opened his mouth without being asked. After placing the thermometer under his tongue, Ray pressed the back of her hand against his forehead. She whistled.

"Wow, you're really hot."

The thermometer beeped and she pulled it out of his mouth. He managed to smile.

"I know but what's my temp?"

Ray's eyes widened as she looked at the display and didn't take the bait of his joke.

"Honey, this says 103.5. We've got to get you to a hospital. Now."

Rory hated hospitals—honestly, who liked them?—but he knew when it was time to stall and when it was necessary to see a professional. He managed to crawl out of bed and slip into some worn sweatpants and an old shirt while Ray ran around the house collecting car keys, jackets, and her purse. She came back to the bedroom.

"Do you need help?"

"No, I got—"

When he stood, pain flashed through his body. It felt like needles dipped in acid then set on fire were dancing a conga line up his spine and into his skull.

Rory collapsed to his knees as the room spun and darkened. Somewhere far away he could hear Ray calling his name. Though he wanted to answer, it was simply easier to let the darkness enfold him.

"Ray?"

Rory called for his wife but the voice that came out of him sounded like his 88-year-old grandpa, Hap, who had smoked three packs of unfiltered cigarettes a day for over fifty years. He cleared his throat and tried again.

"Ray?"

Better but still tainted with gravel. Rory blinked and tried to open his eyes but the light was so bright he could only squint. He tried to raise his hand as a makeshift visor but his arms refused to move. He tilted his head away from the source of the light, a window on his right, and saw his wrist bound in a padded cuff. It looked like one of those bindings used for violent mental patients.

Where the hell was he? Panic pounded in his chest and he screamed.

"Ray! Ray, where are you?"

As he struggled against the restraints, a short blocky woman dressed in pink hospital scrubs rushed into the room.

"Mr. Pearson? Mr. Pearson, calm down."

"Where's Ray? Where's my wife? What's happening?" The nurse pushed a button on the side of the bed.

"You're at Providence Hospital. Mrs. Pearson just went to get some coffee. Don't worry, I'll find her for you."

Two more pink-clad women entered the room and began fussing over him and checking various tubes attached to various machines. The first nurse gave orders to the other two.

"Check his vitals. Change the saline drip as well. I'll page Dr. Wilson and then go find Mrs. Pearson."

Within twenty minutes, Rory was sitting up in bed, sipping water, and staring at the concerned faces of Ray, the stocky nurse, Gina, and Dr. Wilson. According to the doctor, Rory had been unconscious for four days while running an almost constant fever of 105 degrees. No one knew if he'd ever wake up, and judging by the puffy redness of Ray's eyes and face, he'd said as much to prepare her for 'the worst'.

"So what's the diagnosis now, doc?" Rory asked, allowing anger to color his tone.

Ray grabbed Rory's hand, kissed his knuckles, and looked to the doctor.

"Considering you're awake and cognitive, I'd say your prognosis looks good."

Ray let out a huge sigh of relief but the doctor spoke again.

"However, you have to remember, Mr. Pearson, that you were unconscious for some time with a dangerously high fever. We can't rule out even the smallest possibility of brain damage."

"Brain damage?" Ray almost shrieked the question as her fears escalated again and Rory winced. The doctor held up his hands.

"That doesn't always mean something catastrophic, Mrs. Pearson. Since he's awake and talking, I think we can rule out most of the possibilities. But other things, smaller damage, could have occurred."

"Like what?" Rory asked.

"Perhaps some slight memory loss, simple motor function impairment, which we can determine once you get out of bed. Some hearing or vision difficulties, maybe. It's hard to say for sure until we do some tests."

"Do we have to do them today?"

"Oh, no. I think you should spend some time with your wife and rest. Tomorrow will be soon enough."

"Thank you, doctor," Ray said as he smiled at both of them then left the room.

"Why are you thanking him? It's obvious he had you scared to death that I might never recover."

"Oh, Rory. You can't blame him for preparing me.

Besides," she whispered into his ear, "he probably wouldn't want to give me an excuse to sue him."

Rory couldn't help but laugh at that idea then grabbed Ray's waist and pulled her into bed with him.

"Rory! Stop, you shouldn't—"

"Hey, I haven't had my arms around your for four days. I need a dose of Vitamin R."

Ray giggled then relaxed against him, clasping her hands behind his neck.

He jerked with a sudden fear, of what he didn't know, but he felt the need to get her hands off his skin. Rory tried not to let his anxiety show as he pulled her hands off his neck then kissed her palms as a diversion. She smiled. He chalked it up to this illness and leaned back in bed, feeling Ray's head on his chest and her hands firmly clamped in his own.

After two days of tests, observation, and rest, Rory knew two things. One: bacteria had entered his body through the scratch on his hand, resulting in a virulent infection; and two: no obvious notable brain damage could be seen in any of his tests. Though Rory did feel an unfounded anxiety whenever a nurse or doctor would have to touch him for any reason, Dr. Wilson attributed it to the fever and unpleasant nature of being sick in a hospital.

Rory didn't tell him he had the same reaction to his wife's touch because he'd already surmised the same diagnosis.

While Rory dressed, Ray packed up his belongings. Just as he buckled his belt, Dr. Wilson knocked on the door.

"May I come in?"

"Of course," Ray said.

"I just came to get your signature on the release papers so we can get you out of here. How's that sound?"

"Fantastic," Rory said. Doctor Wilson held out a clip board and pen for Rory to take. As he reached for them, the irrational terror popped into his head and he couldn't extend his arms. He thought the doctor's fingers looked like the wicked talons of a medieval dragon. Dr. Wilson frowned.

"Mr. Pearson, are you all right?"

As quickly as the fear came, it faded. Everything looked normal again and Rory shook his head.

"Sorry, Doc. Just tired I guess."

He signed his name and handed the form back to the doctor, who smiled and wished them well.

"You have my card, too, so if anything comes up, please call me."

"I will. Thanks."

After the doctor left, Ray threw the overnight bag filled with Rory's possessions over her shoulder and held her hand out to him.

"Ready to go, sweetie?"

Rory stared at her hand, her dainty fingernails looking like daggers. He choked down his fear, smiled instead, and took her hand in his.

The first three days at home, Rory slept over eighteen hours each day. Every joint ached and he felt depleted, almost like he'd been attacked by that sucker creature from *Star Trek*. Yet by the end of that first week, he felt normal again.

Except for the touching thing. The initial horror he felt at the hospital seemed to intensify with each passing day. Every time he looked at Ray's hands, all he could picture were her nails clawing against his skin, digging into his flesh.

He became so afraid of her touch that he began to avoid her, leaving a room just as she entered, or giving her a wide berth if he couldn't escape soon enough.

Eventually it morphed into a fear of all people touching him. At the liquor store, he loathed to exchange money with cashier; buying a new suit, he shrank away from the salesman helping him into a new jacket; even when his best friend, Andy, extended his hand to shake Rory's, he almost threw up.

"Dude, what is up with you?" Rory shook his head.

"I don't know. Ever since I woke up in that hospital, I've been scared."

"Of what?"

"People touching me. But it's more than that. I just keep imagining everyone will scratch me if they get too close. Even strangers. You should have seen the guy working at McDonalds. When he reached out to take my money, I dropped it and screamed."

"That's weird, dude. Have you talked to the doctor?"

"I've got an appointment to see him tomorrow."

"Ray going?"

"No. I haven't told her any of this."

Andy looked at him with an incredulous smile on his face. Rory laughed. "Yeah, I'm sure she knows, too. But I don't want her to worry any more than she already has."

Andy left it alone and Rory was glad. He didn't want to tell Andy about the other things he was thinking, the things he wanted to do. Rory just hoped the doctor might have some answers.

———

"What kind of brain damage?"

Rory could hear the panic forcing his voice higher. He cleared his throat then repeated the question.

"You see this black shadow near the center of your brain?" Dr. Wilson asked as he pointed to the x-ray film fastened to the light-box behind his desk.

"Yeah."

"That's your amygdala."

"My ami-what?"

"Amygdala. It's the part of the brain that controls our emotions, determines what and where memories are stored, and processing the fear response."

"Looks okay to me."

"Well, it's not supposed to be black. On a normal scan it's more of a light grey."

"Oh."

"Yes. The damage explains the fear you've been experiencing."

"Can you fix it?"

Doctor Wilson sighed.

"I'm sorry, Rory, but I can't. We got rid of the infection that caused it but once the brain is injured, there's nothing we can do."

"So I'll never get better. I'll be afraid. Forever."

"I can prescribe some medications that will suppress those feelings." "But?" Rory felt there was a catch.

"But they would also suppress all of your emotions, could even interfere with your 'fight or flight' instinct—"

"Forget it. I'm already screwed up as it is. I don't want to lose anything else."

Rory stood and slipped on his jacket. The doctor reached out to shake hands and Rory could feel his lip curl in disgust. Dr. Wilson quickly pulled back and mumbled an apology. The fear soured Rory's tongue, almost like the aftertaste of a bad lemon.

"Sorry, Mr. Pearson. I wasn't thinking."

"Right."

As Rory pulled the door open to leave, the doctor called to him.

"Please, Mr. Pearson, call me if you have any questions or a change in your symptoms."

"You bet, doc," Rory yelled over his shoulder.

Of course, he had no intention of doing so. If mind-numbing meds were the only cure, what would Dr. Wilson do if he knew about the urges Rory was having, the hopeful desires he harbored that might 'fix' him? Probably shock therapy. Yeah, the medical staff would stick him in some hospital and juice him with thousands of volts every day. And though that treatment might make him a vegetable, Rory believed he'd still be afraid just locked in an unresponsive body.

Rory walked through the parking lot to his car, hunching his shoulders against the late afternoon chill. A slight drizzle dampened his hair, making him shudder with cold. After getting in his car, a circle of thoughts looped through his mind. Why did he have these problems? Because he had brain damage. What caused the damage? The fever. Why did he have a fever? Because he got an infection. How did he get the infection? Ray scratched him.

Ray. She was the source of all his problems, or more to the point, her nails were.

Those nails. Rory wanted nothing more than to—

He envisioned his next course of action and resolved to put his own cure into motion. That would make him better. It had to. It just had to.

Rory arrived home from his doctor visit at three in the afternoon. Ray wouldn't get home until five so he had plenty of time to prepare. He searched the basement and garage to find the tools and supplies he'd need. It didn't take long, which left him more time to practice his ambush.

At five o'clock sharp, Rory heard Ray's car pull into the driveway. The mechanical rusty shake of the worn garage door vibrated through the walls and into the kitchen, where Rory waited, clutching a short two-by-four plank of wood. The doorway from the garage sat at the end of an el-shaped narrow hallway that ended in the kitchen on Rory's left. As Ray walked through it, she turned away from Rory and toward the dining area.

"Rory? I'm home."

She never saw him, or the piece of wood, before he slammed it against the back of her skull.

By the time she regained consciousness, Rory had dragged Ray down into the basement, tied her to the molasses colored rocking chair she'd inherited from her grandfather, and slapped a long piece of duct tape over her mouth. She stared up at Rory, confusion and some lingering grogginess prevented her from fully comprehending her situation. Once the fog cleared from her head, brought on by her struggle, and failure, to get out of the chair, her eyes widened with fear.

She mumbled something behind the duct tape, probably some kind of inquiry or plea to be released, but Rory shook his head.

"I'm sorry, darling, but I can't understand you. It's okay, though. I'm going to do all the talking. You just need to listen."

Her stare went from his face to the pair of eight-inch steel carpenter's pincers in his hand. Rory lifted them and held them close to her face. She tried to shrink away but her restraints prevented it. He shook them as he spoke, the heavy metal arms clacked together and she flinched with each jarring motion.

"You know, I saw the doctor today. He says I do have brain damage after all. Can you fucking believe it? Brain damage."

She mumbled something again and Rory stepped close to hold the pincers under her nose, but he caught the site of her hands from the corner of his eye and quickly backed away. He could feel the sweat beading down the back of his neck and soaking his t-shirt. He cleared his throat.

"It's not because of the fever, or the infection. It's you, Ray. It's because of you. You and your," he shuddered as he said the words, "filthy nails."

He grabbed her left index finger and clamped the nail in the pincer's grip.

Ray screamed behind the tape as Rory pulled the nail off, leaving a wet bloody patch of flesh at the tip of her finger. Now that he'd done the first one, Rory felt empowered, like he'd just completed the first step of a recovery program. He smiled.

"I'm done talking now."

Rory worked his way through the rest of the nails on her left hand then moved to her right. Ray continued to scream through the entire process, though the tape kept it muffled. Somewhere in the back of his mind Rory thought he should be disgusted with his actions. He was, let's be honest, torturing his wife, the woman he'd loved since high school, the person who had given him so much happiness.

Once he'd finished her hands, Rory knelt down and

yanked off her Mary Janes with such force he heard her ankle bone crack. His stomach did churn at the sound and he almost stopped. Then the thought of her toenails sent the fear into explosive overdrive and he continued.

Ray screamed again but this time it was loud. He looked up and saw a flap of tape hanging off her face. At this point he didn't care if the whole neighborhood heard. He reached up and tore it off, thinking in some bizarre twist of logic it might make her feel better about what he had to do. She probably didn't appreciate the tape taking a few small specs of her skin with it, though.

By the time he finished removing the nails from one foot, Ray had passed out from the pain. She didn't wake up again until he ripped the last nail from her pinkie toe. Ray jerked forward, still trying to free herself from the bindings. She no longer screamed but wept instead, streaks of tears washed down her face and snot bubbled out of her nose. When a long string of saliva slipped past her lips, Rory grimaced.

"I'm so sorry, Ray," Rory said. And he meant it. He didn't really want to hurt her. He just had to ensure she'd never be able to scratch him again. With her nails gone, he felt a great weight had been lifted from his chest. It was only a momentary comfort as he realized that just because his wife couldn't scratch him, it didn't mean no one else would. Or even himself.

He stared down at his fingers and a giant wall of dread crashed down on him, forcing him to his knees. His hands trembled, knowing the pain would be overwhelming, but Rory knew what he had to do. The pincers felt heavy as he clamped them onto his left thumbnail. Silently he counted to three then pulled.

The pain was excruciating, as if he'd dipped his digit in

flaming napalm. He couldn't stop now, though, and forced himself to remove the remaining nineteen nails.

Rory dropped the pincers when he finished and leaned against the wall, tipping his head back and closing his eyes. Already the pain was subsiding and between long ragged gasps he could hear Ray sobbing. He remained silent, the fear crushing his thoughts, making it impossible to comfort her, even though there were no words to offer anyway.

Now that he and Ray were fixed, Rory concentrated on everyone else—his neighbors, family, friends. An entire world filled with people. Seven billion people, with one hundred forty billion nails, waiting to tear at him at any moment when he least expected it.

This won't do, he thought. *I'll never be safe until everyone else is sorted out.* Rory reached over and stroked his wife's hair. Ray continued sobbing, sagging against her restraints. He untied the ropes but she made no move to stand. She simply cried.

"It's all right now, Ray. We can be happy together again. But I'm afraid there are other people out there who can hurt me. So I've got to take care of them, okay?"

He laughed as he grabbed a pair of work gloves from the wall behind his wife.

"I know I can't get everyone in one day but I can make a good start this afternoon. I'll get as far as I can then come back home. Tell you what. I'll even pick up dinner so you don't have to cook."

Ray made no response as Rory kissed the top of her head. "I really am sorry, honey. I'll come back soon."

Once he left the house, Rory didn't know where to start. The bitter cold of winter was keeping people inside. He couldn't barge into people homes, could he? Before he answered his own question, Carl Foster, his next door neighbor, stepped onto his front porch. He was bundled in his daily warm-up suit, knit hat, and fleece gloves, and jogged in place while he fiddled with an iPod. Rory smiled and approached.

Carl came bounding down his front walk and Rory met him halfway. "Hey, Rory. How you feeling, bud—"

Rory pounced on his neighbor. Carl was taken by surprise and it wasn't difficult for Rory to subdue him. Before Carl could slip away, Rory had the man's gloves off and secured one fingernail in the pincer's grip.

"Rory, what the hell are you doing?"

Rory pulled and Carl screamed. Without much of a struggle—perhaps Carl was in shock—Rory removed all of Carl's nails in minutes. He left his neighbor writhing in pain, bleeding from his fingers and toes, and headed up the street.

Another neighbor, John Sellers, ran outside when he heard the screams. Rory jumped him as well, knocking the man down with one right hook, then got to work.

He was able to 'fix' three more neighbors before he realized that removing fingernails wasn't permanent. Even if he could pull them all, they'd grow back.

They'd still be able to hurt him. Then the most brilliant of ideas popped into his head: remove the source of the nails.

Rory had to get back home. He had to handle Ray first then go back through the neighborhood. He could cut off his fingers and toes once he was done. It would be too difficult to hold the pincers otherwise. Except the pincers might not cut through bone. He supposed he could sacrifice one finger to find out.

The pincers, sticky with blood, felt cool against his index finger. He only needed to remove the tip. If he clamped down at the first joint it might be easier. Before he could try, Sookie, a neighborhood English Bulldog, ambled over to him, snorting and wheezing. When Rory watched her approach, he screamed in terror.

He'd forgotten about animals. They all had nails, too, and he was as much in danger from them as from people. He had to get to Sookie. It'd be faster, and easier, to kill her, then he could continue his work. Her tongue lolled out of her mouth and her entire butt wiggled as she came closer. Rory beckoned to her.

"That's right, Sookie. Come here, girl. I got a treat for you."

When she was within reach, he tried to lunge at her but his body refused to move forward. Rory turned his head and was shocked to see two police officers holding his arms. Their bare hands gripped him and he shrieked, thrashing and trying to pull loose. He heard a strange crackling noise, felt a sharp pain against his neck, and everything went black.

———

Rory faded in and out of consciousness. He didn't know the day, time, or place. He only registered men and women in white uniforms, the small pinch of a needle in his arm, and the soft floating feeling of narcotics. At one point he thought he saw Ray looking at him through a small window of a grey door, her face red and puffy the way it looked when she had been crying for a long time. Then he drifted away again.

Rory awoke to the screech of rusty hinges. He opened his eyes and saw white ceiling tiles, white padded walls, and a man in a white uniform wheeling a small rickety cart. The man stopped next to Rory and looked down at him.

"Good morning, Mr. Pearson. How are we feeling today?"

"Gugh?" was all Rory could say. He tried to sit up but his body felt cocooned. He looked down to see a yellow stained straight jacket wrapped around him. Panic tripped his heartbeat into overdrive and Rory finally realized where he was: a mental hospital. They must have brought him here when—

Oh god. They stopped him before he could fix everyone. Fix himself. He could feel his fingernails growing, extending into claws that would rip through the rough fabric of the jacket and pierce his flesh. He had to get out of here. He struggled to sit up.

"Whoa, whoa. Hold on there, Mr. Pearson," the man said as he gripped Rory's shoulders. "Just settle down and I'll give you some happy pills, all right?"

"You don't understand," Rory said. "I can feel them. They're growing."

The orderly sat on the edge of the bed.

"What's growing, Mr. Pearson?"

"My fingernails. They're growing. So are Ray's, Carl's, even..."

"Even what, Mr. Pearson?" the man asked when Rory grew silent.

"Yours."

"Mine? My fingernails, you mean? My nails are fine. Look."

He held up his hands and Rory could see the blackened claws extending from the fingertips, ragged but sharp. He tried to recoil but the man shoved his hand closer.

"What do you see, you nut case? Do my nails scare you? Oooooo!"

He laughed and wiggled his fingers in Rory's face.

Instinct took over and Rory threw his head forward, butting his forehead against the man's nose. The man yelped and fell backward, onto the floor. Rory's legs had not been bound so he leaped from his bed and sat atop the orderly who held his hands against his broken nose. He mumbled curses at Rory.

Rory didn't have a tool, or even free hands, to remove the man's nails so what could he do? When the man reached forward to push Rory away, Rory did the first thing that came to mind. He opened his mouth and clamped down on the orderly's finger. His teeth found the first joint and Rory squeezed his jaw as hard as he could. The tip of the man's finger came away easily and Rory spit it out onto the floor; it seemed he had the best tool for the job all along. He could feel blood drip down his chin as he smiled at the terrified man beneath him. Rory gnashed his teeth and the orderly screamed.

"How are you today, Earl?"

The older man looked up at the slim, pretty blonde woman as he scanned her ticket into the computer.

"Just fine, Emily. How are you?"

"Well, the sun is shining, there's a nice breeze, and I'm playing hooky from work to watch a baseball game. Could be worse."

Earl smiled and nodded. "Yes, it could. Enjoy the game."

"Thanks, Earl. Take care."

Emily headed towards her seat section with her friend, chatting away about shoes or some such nonsense. Earl studied her behind as it swayed with each step she took. He licked his lips, imagining the delicious things he could do with it.

Once the game was over and all the park employees had cleaned up their workstations and punched out on the time clock, Earl ambled out to the parking lot. He may have been seventy years old but he was still a good driver. He'd restored a red and white 1959 Cadillac El Dorado Biarritz to cherry condition. Not only was it a classic car but it had the most trunk space of any vehicle made at the time.

He pulled the car into his garage and entered the kitchen, shrugging off his park jacket and hanging it on a hook by the side door. He eased off his orthopedic support shoes and pushed his feet into a pair of UGG slippers. Yes, he was too old for such trendy fashions but they sure were warm and soft for his sore feet.

He filled the teakettle with water and put it on the stove. He picked up his worn woolen sweater, slipping his arms into its familiar comfort. While he waited for the water to heat up, he made his way to the living room and sat in his easy chair.

Earl looked around at the décor. After his beloved wife died ten years ago, he finally got the chance to decorate the house as he wanted. The bookshelf on his right, holding eight jars with severed heads floating in formaldehyde, was dark cherry wood—his favorite. The matching coffee table, covered with the tanned and stretched skins of four different young women, showed a few nicks and scratches but was in otherwise pristine condition.

He reached for the TV remote which sat in a skeletal hand cut from his last victim, a young brunette he'd met at the grocery store. It amazed him how easy it was to fool trusting, naïve young women into thinking he was a harmless old man.

The kettle whistled from the kitchen just as Jeopardy went to a commercial. "Time for tea," Earl muttered.

He shuffled back to the kitchen and grabbed a clean mug from the dish rack next to the sink. A box of his favorite cinnamon tea sat open on the counter and he plucked a bag free. He dropped it into the mug and covered it with hot water. As he left it to steep, Earl studied the pictures of Emily he'd hung on the refrigerator: at the ballpark, her work, the mall, and her home.

"There'll be time enough for you too, my dear," he whispered.

IT'S NOT WHAT YOU THINK

Patty recited the Apostle's Creed to begin praying the rosary. As she moved on to the Our Father, her voice became part of the chorus created by the rest of her fifth grade class. She didn't know why they had to pray the rosary today but being a student at Holy Name Catholic School meant she had to do a lot of praying, and penance, and other church stuff she never really understood.

By the time the class started on the first set of Hail Mary's, Patty's mouth moved on auto pilot. This was the fourth time this month the thirty-three students knelt in the small church adjacent to the school. Either they all committed a lot of sins or the teachers believed they did. Whatever the case, Patty thought it was all very silly.

And boring.

As the words tumbled out of her mouth, their meaning and purpose lost, Patty looked around the church. The altar, draped with a white and gold cloth and adorned with fat white candles, sat at the front of the church. A ten-foot tall crucified Jesus hung above it, his body bloody and his face a mask of agony. Patty shivered.

She turned her head to the left toward the confessionals. The dark brown wood always gave Patty the creeps. It reminded her of the inside of her dentist's office. Dr. Rosen always ruffled her hair or touched her hands or kissed her on the cheek, telling her what a big girl she was.

Blech!

Patty stared at the confessional and it seemed like the lights dimmed. The wood darkened to black and the nearby Stations of the Cross lost their details. Then she realized the walls, the floor, everything had blurred. The church wasn't getting darker; her eyesight was fading. Just as blackness swallowed the entire building, little grey and white dots fluttered across her vision, like when the cable went out. Her mom called it 'the ant races' though Patty never could see a resemblance to the creepy crawlers.

She swiveled her head back and forth until finally her sight began to clear. A wave of nausea rolled through her stomach. Her face felt hot as her body shook with cold. Patty looked over at her teacher, Mrs. Whitehill. The woman looked panicked as she stared back at her student.

"I don't feel well," Patty mouthed. Mrs. Whitehill pointed to the exit, indicating Patty go out into the small alcove as soon as possible. She did, wobbling a little as she stood, then shuffled out of the church.

The fresh air blowing through the outside doorway into the alcove did not help her feel better as she expected. If anything, the simple act of putting one foot in front of the other made her stomach flop again. The breeze blew against her face and she realized she was sweating. As it cooled her skin, she got the shivers again. All Patty wanted to do was lie down, perhaps vomit. But not in that order.

Mrs. Whitehill entered the recess, her face still pinched with worry. She put a hand on Patty's shoulder.

"You don't look well, Patty. I thought you were going to faint."

The slight pressure of her teacher's hand felt like a concrete block pushing her ribcage into her abdomen. Patty's stomach rolled again.

"You'd better go to the office. I'll have one of your classmates go with you."

Patty nodded. She waited in the alcove until Mrs. Whitehill returned with Molly McGuire.

"Molly, please take Patty to the office. The Secretary can call her parents, all right?"

"Yes, Mrs. Whitehill. C'mon, Patty."

Molly took Patty's arm and though it didn't press on her like the teacher's hand had, Patty felt the nausea rise to the back of her throat. She let Molly lead her through the school toward the main office. Just before they reached it, Patty heaved.

Clamping a hand over her mouth, Patty dashed into the nearest bathroom. She ignored Molly's inquiries and shoved the closest stall door open, not bothering to close or lock it behind her.

Patty bent over the toilet and heaved but nothing came up. He stomach lurched and she opened her mouth. Again, nothing. She continued to dry heave for five minutes. When her stomach stopped churning and she realized she wasn't going to have the full technicolor yawn, Patty straightened.

She moved slowly to the sink and splashed some cold water on her face. Though she did feel a bit better, Patty took her time leaving the bathroom just in case she had to vomit for real.

"Patty, are you okay?"

Patty nodded, not trusting her throat to produce any audible sounds. When she looked up at Molly, Patty could see shadowy figures down the hall behind her. When she focused, Patty saw her best friend, Jo, being half dragged, half carried down the hall.

The two students on either side of Jo appeared to be struggling with the weight of their burden. It's not every day that fifth graders were expected to haul their fellow students around, wounded-warrior style. All the pull-ups in gym class can't prepare a bunch of ten year olds for something like this.

Jo's knees buckled and all three students almost tumbled to the floor. At the last moment, the kid on the left, Jocelyn, pulled Jo to her feet and the second helper, Lana, was able to stabilize them all. They continued their shuffle-drag-walk toward Patty.

Once Patty reached the office, her head began to clear. Her nausea dissipated and the fuzzy edge around her vision cleared. It almost felt as if a heavy blanket had been lifted off her head and by the time her dad arrived at the school to take her home, Patty felt fine, as if she'd never been sick at all.

As she left the office, Patty looked back at Jo and she, too, looked better than she had as she shuffled down the hallway just fifteen minutes earlier. As her dad mumbled something about faking it, Patty wondered if something in the church had made them sick.

After assigning several students to help Patty and Jo get to the main office, Mrs. Whitehill went back into the church, instructing the remaining students to continue with the rosary prayers. Just as she knelt to join them, yet another student, Paul Barton, collapsed. Before she could even move, the other teacher, Miss Garbo, began to panic.

"Why are these children getting sick while praying?"

"Relax, Mary," Mrs. Whitehill said. "Maybe—"

"They must be under some kind of satanic influence."

Mrs. Whitehill blinked.

"What?"

"None of the other students have been affected. And you know those two other girls are as thick as thieves."

"What are you talking about?"

Miss Garbo's hands fluttered to the gold cross at her throat. Mrs. Whitehill always thought the young woman a bit overzealous in her beliefs, even for a Catholic school teacher. Her youth and naiveté didn't help matters.

"I heard them talking about the devil on several occasions. And that boy," she pointed at Paul who now lay across the pew, "was with them and laughing. It's the devil, I tell you. The devil is in them."

"Mary, calm down. I think you're overreacting just a bit."

"Really?" the younger teacher screeched, causing the remaining students to pause in their recitations. They all stared at the two teachers. Miss Garbo continued.

"Do you see any of the other students getting sick?"

"No, but,"

"But nothing! They've brought the devil here!"

"Mary, stop it!" Mrs. Whitehill yelled. "You're scaring the students."

Mrs. Whitehill stared over the thirty children, all of whom looked at her or Miss Garbo with a bright fear in their eyes. The students closest to Paul began to move away from him, leaving the poor boy slumped in an awkward position on the hard wooden bench. Mrs. Whitehill bent down next to him and laid him across the length of the pew. He remained unconscious but at least his head wasn't twisted to the side anymore.

"They should be scared," Miss Garbo said. "Satan is among them, among us, and it's because of those two girls and him!"

The children began to whimper and cry. Not because they truly understood the meaning of evil and Satan, Mrs. Whitehill suspected, but because Miss Garbo was whipping them into a fervor of terror just with her voice and body language.

"Mary, stop this! Let's just think about it for a minute."

Mrs. Whitehill surveyed the area around and near the pew where Paul lay. He and the two girls were kneeling here, a bit separated from the rest of the class. Mrs. Whitehill studied the wall to the left and saw the clunky and half rusted rectangular faces of several older gas powered heating units. Sometimes in the colder months, like now, the church set these up around the nave to help take some of the chill out of the air. Perhaps the one closest to the pews was broken.

Mrs. Whitehill walked toward the heater but after only a few steps, the smell of gas overwhelmed her. She felt dizzy then quickly stepped away and her head began to clear. She smiled to herself, relieved that she could explain the three children's symptoms.

Mrs. Whitehill turned back to the class and Miss Garbo.

"It's a gas leak, Mary. Can't you smell it? Those three kids were kneeling right next to a gas—"

Miss Garbo spun toward the children and pointed at Mrs. Whitehill.

"She's with them, children. She's with the devil! Don't you dare believe her lies!"

The students moved away from Mrs. Whitehill, some of them crying, some confused but not wanting to appear stupid and so they moved with their classmates, and others stared at her with a malevolence that frightened her. They looked angry, hateful, and deadly.

One student, James Doherty, one of the more brazen and rebellious of the class, stepped toward Mrs. Whitehill and spat at her, the glob of saliva landing on her shoe with a wet plop. Even for a child with a rambunctious history, she stared at him in disbelief. Then a few of his friends joined in.

Mrs. Whitehill backed away as several more students closed in on her, spitting or spewing insults and curses. For a group of ten year olds they surprised her with their knowledge of such a variety of vulgarities.

"Bitch."

"Devil's whore."

"Slut bag."

"Satan fucker."

"Cunt."

That last curse was one she rarely heard adults use, let alone children. As she tried to ascertain who said it, a hymnal flew at her and smacked against her temple. The dizziness returned, not from the gas leak but from pain. The first tendrils of dread gripped Mrs. Whitehill as she realized that even though these were merely children, there were thirty of them and they were united in the group-think of fear. She was in real danger.

Another hymnal sailed in her direction. She dodged it but as she recovered, a third hit her square in the face and she heard and felt her nose break. Blackness closed in at the edges of her vision and she collapsed to her knees. She looked up to see Miss Garbo standing behind the children as they moved forward, each with a thick heavy hymnal or clenched fists. The twisted grin on Mary's face chilled Mrs. Whitehill's blood.

Before she could fathom why Miss Garbo has done this, one of the students hit Mrs. Whitehill across the back of her head. White dots of pain sprinkled the space in front of her and she folded forward. The last things she saw were the black school mandated shoes of thirty students as they descended upon her in a murderous fury.

When they'd finished, the children stepped away from the gruesome heap of the now dead Mrs. Whitehill. Those students holding bloody hymn books dropped them and the combined cacophony echoed through the small church like approaching thunder. Most looked down at their teacher's corpse with incredulity, either in their ability to kill or the woman's death specifically, Miss Garbo couldn't tell. Whatever the case, she smiled, pleased at how easy it was to manipulate them. As the children turned to look at her, she tried to soften her expression from malicious glee to sympathy.

"It's all right, children. You did well. God would be pleased."

"But Miss Garbo, we killed her. We killed Mrs. Whitehill!"

Mary looked at the student, Laura, as she began to cry.

"But you did it to defeat Satan. For God's glory."

Laura began to wail then knelt beside Mrs. Whitehill's body. The little girl, so fierce only minutes ago, appeared fragile and scared. She pushed at the corpse as if trying to wake the dead teacher.

"Please, Mrs. Whitehill. I'm sorry. I didn't mean to. Get up now, okay? Please get up."

Two other girls began to cry as well and knelt down next to Laura. Miss Garbo mentally rolled her eyes and pushed her plan to the next stage.

"You're with her, aren't you? You and those other children. You all want to see the devil succeed!"

Her voice cracked with a shriek and all three girls stood, shaking their heads in denial. But Miss Garbo has already planted the seeds of deception. The remaining students advanced on the girls, eager now to satiate their awakened bloodlust.

Within the hour, all but two of the students were dead, Mary having turned them against each other with accusations. Only James and his friend, Theodore, remained, the two of them doing most of the killing with a brutality belying their tender age. It would be a shame to have to destroy that budding talent but Mary could leave no survivors of the morning's activities.

Yes, a handful of students had escaped because of a real gas leak, which Miss Garbo had created to get the ball rolling. Once rumors leaked out, however, of the horrors of Mrs. Whitehill's satanic worship and the convenient survival of Patty, Jo, and the helper students, they and their families wouldn't survive for long. The rest of society would see to that.

Miss Garbo laughed, long and loud, as James and Theo stared at her. They chuckled softly with her, not noticing the six-inch silver blade that Mary slipped from the hidden sheath at her back. Still laughing, she reached her left arm toward James, pulling him into an embrace, then jammed the knife deep into his heart, killing him instantly.

As he dropped to the floor, Mary grinned at Theo. His shock rooted him in place and he didn't even attempt to save himself as Mary slashed his throat in one swift movement. He collapsed to the floor, his mouth snapping open and shut like a fresh fish on a butcher's block. As he slowly bled out, Mary sheathed the knife then knelt into the pool of spreading blood. She covered her hands in the viscous fluid then moved to the floor in front of the altar.

Kneeling down, she began to paint an archaic symbol across the grey marble, sweeping arcs and swirling lines blended together as she recited an ancient text of summoning. Though to any on-looker, the church appeared normal (aside from the piled corpses of children, of course). But to Mary, a bright white light filled the chancel and a percussive wave of energy flew through the church, knocking over pews, the baptismal font, candle stands, and lectern. Mary closed her eyes and laughed in ecstasy.

"Lucifer, the time has come for your glory. I have begun the cycle with these sacrifices. All will tremble in the sight of your power!"

A deep soothing voice filled the church.

"You have done well, my child. The foolish humans will look for the signs given them in their Bible but will not find them. We will install ourselves through quiet whispers, not bloody rivers; we will secure our power with falsehoods and subtle machinations, not martyrs and horsemen. By the time they realize their fates, that I was right all along to reject their superiority, it will be too late."

"Their blood will paint the walls of your temples. Their bones will adorn your throne. Their souls will feed your majesty!"

"Go now, daughter. Go out into the world and prepare for my coming."

"As you wish, Father."

The light faded and the church settled back into a hushed stillness. Mary stood and surveyed the carnage in the nave. She'd have to hide the massacre from the public. She flicked her hands in multiple directions, snapping gas lines and allowing the flammable vapor to fill the church. While the ensuing inferno would at first be considered a terrible tragedy, Miss Garbo would begin the rumors, allowing the public to tap into their own paranoid fears. What humanity would believe to be actions for the grace of God would merely be the awakening of their own flawed natures. They would destroy themselves through no faults but their own.

Miss Garbo walked to the back of the church, heading for the narthex and then the exit. She pushed open the tall heavy doors and stepped out into the fading morning sun. Thick puffy clouds swarmed together creating a heavy barrier and blocking the sun's rays. Already the air was beginning to chill.

Mary turned to push the doors closed. She looked over the butchery spread throughout the church and laughed.

"The meek, my ass."

She slammed the doors closed then left. When she'd walked several blocks away, she snapped her fingers. A small votive candle in the south transept inside the church flickered to life. Seconds later the building disappeared in an explosion of brick, wood, and marble. A pillar of flame shot into the sky and a black tower of smoke joined the rising cumulonimbus clouds in blotting out the sun.

Mary smiled and disappeared with the fading light.

A ROSE BY ANY OTHER NAME

Rose slouched over her phone protectively, cradling it in the crook of her arm as she spoke. As one of her co-workers walked past her desk, she angrily slammed her hand down on the notepad and pencil lying next to her computer. She tucked the receiver under her chin as she turned to give the evil eye to the passer-by. It was Neil, one of the sales reps whose cube was down the hall from hers. He cringed in fear and quickened his pace, trying not to make direct eye contact.

Rose went back to her phone call. "I'm sorry but Mr. Charles is out for the rest of the afternoon. Would you like to leave him a message? Yes, he does have voice mail. I'll put you right in there. You're welcome. Have a nice day."

Rose slammed the receiver down on her desk several times before punching the buttons to transfer the caller into the voice mail system. After her sugary sweet-talk only moments before, the caller must have been extremely puzzled as to what he could have done to deserve having his eardrum punctured by her angry display.

Cocksuckers all of them, Rose thought to herself. If it

wasn't the goddamned sales reps calling, it was the accounting department. If it wasn't them, it was Travel. If it wasn't them, it was the mailroom. Someone needed to meet with Mr. Charles. Someone else needed a shipping label filled out. He needed a meeting with the client or she needed her expense report typed up.

Rose jabbed her pencil on her notepad, scrawling out a 'to do' list. So far she had ten items listed and was adding two more. She hadn't gotten a chance to finish any of them yet and it was already 10:15am. If the goddamned phone would just stop ringing, and if people would just stop coming to her cube to interrupt her, she'd be able to get some work done.

Just this morning she'd had two of her people, Phil and Becky, complain to her about meeting screw-ups. Apparently it was Rose's fault that Becky forgot to invite her coworkers to the meeting. Never mind that Becky should have counted herself lucky that Rose was able to get the client's cooperation. It also seemed to be Rose's fault that the other meeting, which Phil set up himself but didn't tell her about or involve her in any way, had changed times. She just happened to notice a time conflict on Phil's calendar, called the client's secretary to confirm the meeting time, and corrected it on the calendar. Naturally, Phil thought she screwed it up.

If one more person came to her today and complained about one more thing, any little thing, she was going to lose it. For 16 years she'd worked at this prominent advertising firm in Detroit. 16 years of the same shit, day after day, week after week. For only $28,000 a year, it just wasn't worth the effort anymore. She was expected to be a mind reader, hostess, meeting regulator, diplomat, waitress, cleaning woman, gofer, computer genius, travel agent, golf coordinator—all along with her regular duties as a secretary like copying, filing, answering phones, and typing.

"Rose, I need you to change those flights again for my trip on Monday."

"Rose, I know it's 4:30 but I want you to set up a meeting with the CEO and all 12 members of our team for first thing tomorrow morning."

"Rose, you've got to make sure you remind me to send that document over to the client."

"Rose, I need 20 copies of this 100-page report by lunch —and don't forget to put the copies in 3-ring binders, with colored tabs."

"Rose, I want this.....Rose, I need that....Rose, you better get going on these..."

The tip of her pencil snapped in the middle of writing her twelfth 'to do' task. It spun backwards and jabbed her in the eye. Her hand flew to her face.

Luckily the lead point just bounced off her eyelashes and didn't actually embed in her eye. But it started to water and soon droplets of saline streaked down her face.

As she held her hand over her eye she could almost hear the dry twig snap of her mind breaking down. Her body spasmed once, jerked to the left, and she hiccuped. She slowly lowered her hand and let it fall slack at her side. A curious smile curled her lips and her face flushed a soft pink. Sighing, she looked around her desk and cube, searching for just the right tool.

Carolyn, one of the coordinators that Rose worked for, walked up to her just as Rose lifted the razor-sharp metal ruler from her desk. She glanced at Carolyn and smiled.

"Rose, I think you forgot to set up that..."

In a bright flash the metal ruler sliced across Carolyn's face. A two-inch gash slowly opened on her right cheek and dripped bright red blood down her jaw line. She opened her mouth in surprise, which stretched the gash open even further. Her perfectly white molars sparkled through, darkened only slightly by a few smudges of blood.

As Carolyn studied the bloodstains dripping onto her blouse in horror, Rose struck again. She slashed and sliced, over and over, at every piece of exposed flesh she could find. Carolyn shrieked and raised her arms in defense but Rose ripped them to shreds with the ruler. Carolyn collapsed on the floor, meekly holding up her arms and curling into a fetal position. Rose continued to strike blow after blow. The tearing of fabric and flesh echoed through the office and blood spattered the floor, the walls, and Rose.

By the time Rose finished with her, Carolyn looked like she had gone through the shredder. Her clothes lay in crimson and soggy tatters around her mutilated corpse. The carpet squished around her body. What flesh had been missed in the rage was slick and shiny with blood. Rose bent down next to what used to be a human being and poked it, lifting a flap of ruined skin, gouging the ruler into various cuts, measuring their depths. She dropped the ruler on the floor and stood, using the sleeve of her blouse to remove Carolyn's blood from her face.

Neil, the sales rep who'd passed by Rose's desk only moments ago, came running back when he heard Carolyn's screams. He pulled up short only inches from the pile of flesh that was Carolyn and gagged. He clamped his hand over his mouth in horror and stared at Rose. She was still smiling, but the smudges of blood remaining on her face made her look like a tribal warrior ready for the next death match. She hefted a heavy-duty stapler in her hands, bouncing it up and down as if testing the weight.

Neil's eyes widened and he backed up a step. Rose

stepped forward. Neil raised his foot to step back again but Rose lifted a finger and shook it at him.

"Tsk. Tsk. Tsk....Neil."

His name on her lips sounded like the whisper of death and he froze in fear.

She lifted the stapler, which was about three or four pounds of clunky metal and sharp corners, and bashed Neil at his left temple. His glasses flew off his face as he collapsed to the floor. The pain blinded him for a moment. Rose stood over him, holding the stapler high above her head. Only when he turned to look up at her did she bring the stapler down to his face.

He didn't have time to scream. The bottom of the hefty stapler crushed his nose into his face on the first blow. Teeth and blood spurted from his mouth. Bone crunched wetly. Rose straddled Neil, lifted the stapler and brought it down to his face again. More bone splintered. Blood and brains squirted out his ears. She lifted the stapler again and again, slamming it into Neil's face over and over until it resembled a mixture of mashed fruit and lumpy oatmeal.

She dropped the stapler and stood, her knees popping. She walked past the secretary, Mary, who sat next to her. She was in her late 50's and had been at the company longer than Rose. Mary looked at her in wide-eyed surprise and awe. Rose stepped over to her, patted her on the shoulder, and whispered in her ear.

"Why don't you take the rest of the day off, Mary. Sound good?"

Mary nodded quickly and grabbed her coat and bag. She gave Rose a quick half-smile and hurried out to the elevators. Rose smiled back and looked around Mary's desk. She spotted the speakerphone and grinned. She removed the phone cord and pulled it taught between her hands, wrapping the slack into her fists.

Suddenly two large arms wrapped around her from behind. She twisted her head to the side and saw Mark, the department director, grimacing to hold her steady while she struggled to free herself. He was about 6'2" and 260 pounds but his instep was just as sensitive as any baby's. Rose ground her heel into his foot and he yelped in pain. He released her and she spun around, kneeing him in the nuts. A small girlish squeak whistled past his lips and he fell to his knees, cupping his damaged balls tenderly. Rose swiftly stepped behind him and stretched the phone cord over his neck. She pulled back with all her might, leaning back with all her 180 pounds.

Mark immediately forgot about his privates and reached up to his throat. His fingers scrabbled for the cord, but he couldn't get under it. His eyes bulged as the capillaries popped and the whites filled with blood. A string of spittle hung from his lower lip and it swung back and forth every time he gasped for air.

In minutes his hands stopped fumbling for the cord and fell to his sides. His body relaxed in death and he slumped forward. Rose held the cord in place for another minute, letting Mark's own weight crush his windpipe completely. She released the cord and Mark dropped to the floor with a heavy thud. Rose looked around to see if anyone else was planning to interrupt her work. The office was empty.

Apparently, taking out Mark was enough to convince everyone that Rose was no one to be fucked with today. She heard the soft 'ding' of the elevator down the hall. Stepping over Mark's body she walked down the hall to the double doors that lead to the bank of elevators. Her supervisor, Mr. Charles, stepped out of the farthest elevator and walked away from her. He turned left and headed to his office in the corner on the other side of the floor.

If she hurried, Rose could cut him off by turning back the way she'd come, cut through the small kitchen, haul ass to the right, and catch him before he reached the safety of his office. As she sprinted down the hall she heard him call out.

"Where the hell is everybody? Isn't anyone working today?"

Just as he approached his office door, Rose exploded out of the adjoining hallway and rushed him. She barreled into him and slammed him into the door. The knob jammed into his right kidney and knocked the wind out of him.

Temporarily disabled, he just stood there, not defending himself. She reached behind him, threw open the door, and pushed him to his office floor.

As he lay there, stunned, Rose slammed his office door. The force of it blew the glass paneling from the wall, leaving jagged pieces clinging in the frame. She pried one loose, slicing her palm. Unaffected, she walked to her prone, but less dazed supervisor, and jammed the glass shard into his left shoulder.

The pain brought him to full awareness and he screamed in agony, the shard scraping along his collarbone with each breath. She stood over him, pressing her finger against the glass edge protruding from his shoulder. He screamed again. His eyes rolled up into his head as if he was about to pass out from the pain. She flicked the glass shard hard and he snapped to full attention once again.

His eyes swam briefly and finally locked on hers. He frowned. He hadn't fully comprehended that she was the source of his suffering.

"Wha...? Rose? What happened? What's going on?"

"What's going on?" she mimicked. "What's going on? I'll tell you what's going on, Mr. Charles. It's payback time. You're going to pay me back for all the shit you and your lemmings have put me through for the last 16 years."

She grabbed his desk chair and rolled it over to him. He struggled to get away but as soon as he twitched his arm muscle, a hot spasm of pain laced up his neck and back down to his wounded shoulder. He laid back on the floor, the pain draining his energy away too quickly.

No sooner did he close his eyes, than Rose gripped him beneath his shoulders and hefted him onto the chair. His entire left side was a parade of fire ants. He tentatively reached for the glass shard in his shoulder but Rose quickly slapped his hand away and then wiggled the shard to make her point. Tears streamed down his face as he watched Rose circle his chair. Her arms were folded across his chest as she spoke.

"Now, Mr. Charles. We're going to straighten a few things out, you and I. I've been working for this company, and you, for 16 years. There have been good times and bad times and I've enjoyed my tenure here for the most part. But recently, it has come to my attention that you're all a bunch of fucks."

"Rose, please..." Mr. Charles pleaded.

She slapped him hard across the face. "No interruptions. You've had your time in the driver's seat, Mr. Charles. Now it's my turn. Where was I?"

She paused and looked at him, her eyes burning with intense rage. He cleared his throat gingerly.

"Uh...we're a bunch of fucks."

"Ah, yes. Thank you, Mr. Charles. That's one point in your favor. Unfortunately, you're about 3 bazillion in the red right now so it doesn't help much, does it? As I was saying, you're all completely worthless. I had an epiphany this morning, Mr. Charles. I realized that none of you are contributing anything worthwhile to the world. All you can do is whine, complain, point fingers, slack off, bilk the company out of money you didn't earn, sneak, lie, cheat, and act like you've all got the sun shining out of your asses. Now what kind of human being would I be if I let that continue?"

She leaned over him placing her hands on either armrest and breathed heavily into his face.

"How could you let things come to this, Mr. Charles? How could you let your people get so out of control?"

"But, Rose, if you were unhappy, why didn't you tell me?"

Her left eyelid twitched. Her face flushed from bright red to deep purple and she gripped the armrests of his chair with fierce anger.

"Why didn't....Why didn't I..."

She screeched at the top of her lungs and pushed forward. She ran with Mr. Charles, and his chair, straight at the window facing Heart Plaza and the Spirit of Detroit. Unbelievably, the window cracked slightly.

"When exactly was I supposed to come to you, Mr. Charles? Would that be before your morning golf game, or after your late lunch or sometime during your after work drinks with the clients?"

She rammed his chair against the window again and the crack widened, zigzagging up and out.

"Should I have interrupted you during your bi-weekly screw of the catering supervisor or maybe on your way to the local hooker for a blow-job that you paid for after raiding the petty cash drawer?"

The shock on his face made Rose howl with laughter.

She pulled his chair away from the window and his face relaxed. Unfortunately for him, she was only moving him back so she could take another run at the window with him. She charged forward and this time, a huge chunk of glass blew out of the window and spiraled down twelve floors to the street.

A crisp cool breeze wafted through the hole in the window. She pushed her boss and his chair to the side. Closing her eyes she let the soft wind blow through her hair and dry the sweat on her face. A peaceful calm washed over her. She turned to her boss.

"It's time for you to go now, Mr. Charles."

Whimpering, he tried to make a dash for the door but the pain in his shoulder left him breathless and he couldn't manage more than a twitch. Rose grabbed him by his shirt and hefted him to his feet. He screamed in agony as she jostled him towards the broken window. She slammed him against the remnants of glass and they shattered from the pane and fell to the street.

Still holding on to his shirt, she pushed him backwards until the top half of his body was hanging out in the open air. Bending over she leaned him more and more precariously over the bustling city sidewalk twelve stories below. She kissed him on the cheek and smiled sweetly.

"Good bye, Mr. Charles."

She let go of his shirt and his body tumbled backwards. She wiggled her fingers in good-bye, smirking in satisfaction. In a last ditch effort to save himself, Mr. Charles grabbed her shirtsleeve. As his center of gravity tumbled over the window's edge, his body weight pulled an extremely surprised Rose out through the opening. They both plummeted twelve stories to the sidewalk. When the police arrived, it was difficult for them to decipher which parts belonged to Rose and which belonged to Mr. Charles.

Hours later, several police officers were taping off the 12th floor to keep out the morbidly curious and to preserve evidence.

"Hey, Bill. Did you talk to any of the witnesses?"

"Yeah, Rob, I did. Most of them are pretty shaken up but they all said that this woman just went nuts. Always kept to herself, was kind of a loner. I guess she was pretty quiet for the most part. Until today, that is."

Rob shook his head.

"It's always the quiet ones."

HERE THERE BE MONSTERS

"Will you move?"

"Why don't you?"

"You're on my side, you know."

"I don't see your name. Is there a line drawn to show where your side starts and mine stops?"

He drew an imaginary line on the floor between himself and his sister.

"There. That's your side and this is mine."

"You are such a larva."

"I am not."

"Are too."

"Am not!"

The argument continued until their mother called to them. "Hey! What's going on up there?"

"Mom, Antora said I was a larva."

"Well, he keeps whining."

"Antora, Geluven, stop fighting. Do not make me come up there. Now, don't you have a job to do?"

"But he," Antora sputtered.

"But she," Geluven whined.

"Enough! You two asked to help and now you've been given a job. Maybe your father and I were too hasty in trusting you."

"No!" Antora yelled. "We'll do it. We'll stop fighting."

Their mother waited for her son's response. When he didn't speak up, she called again.

"Geluven?"

"Yes," he mumbled. "I can't hear you."

Antora rammed her fist into his third eye. "Ow!"

"What was that?"

"Yes, Mother, all right. We'll stop fighting."

"That's better. Now get to it."

Antora smiled at her brother, a temporary truce enacted long enough to finish their job. Geluven nodded at her then she turned her attention to the bed frame above them.

Pushing her top arms against the cross bar, Antora felt its sturdy construction. Her lower arms reached to either side to test the frame's fabrication strength.

As she did that, Geluven used the sharpened talons on his hands and feet to shred the cloth covering on the box spring. The tearing sound pulsed a tickling sensation on Antora's vesicles and she smiled at her brother.

"How long do you think it will take for you to get through?"

He shrugged. "Not sure. Depends on how thick this thing is. Why?"

"This frame is well assembled. I'm not sure if I can break it apart."

"All right. I'll go as fast as I can."

Antora nodded. "In the meantime, I'll give him a little preview."

Geluven smiled and Antora grabbed the sides of the frame with her four hands. She pushed with all her strength and the bed lifted a few inches off the floor. A quiet whimper floated down from above them.

"Ha! Got him," she whispered to her brother. "But I'm definitely not strong enough to break this thing. You'll have to get him through the bedding."

"All right. You keep shaking it, though. It'll keep him distracted until I tear through."

Antora nodded but before she could continue, Geluven looked at her. "Ever wonder why we have to take them through the bed? Why can't we just reach around and grab them?"

"Geluven," Antora tried to interrupt him but he kept talking.

"Or better yet, get out from under here and pounce on 'em? Wouldn't that be faster?"

"Geluven! What is the First Rule?"

He stuck out his bottom lips in a pout as he recited the most important rule of their society.

"Be heard not seen above the ground. Death to all if one is found."

"Exactly. Do you want to risk getting trapped up here? Do you know what will happen if the humans find just one of us? Do you want to be responsible for killing us all?"

"No."

"I didn't think so. Now let's get back to work."

Geluven agreed and Antora braced her legs underneath the frame along with her lower arms. She pushed up and down, causing the bed to shake like hers did during a magma disturbance. The human on the top side started to cry.

"Mommy!"

Antora looked at Geluven.

"Hurry up," she hissed. "Once the parental unit arrives, we may lose our chance."

He doubled his efforts but pulled back his hand when he hit the core. A loop of metal twanged and snapped, breaking one of his talons and piercing his thick skin. Geluven stuck the injured digit in his mouth.

"Ow! What was that?"

"That was a spring. Remember what Father said? He knew this could happen since your scales haven't fully generated yet. Are you all right?"

Geluven looked at his hand and Antora saw a shallow cut. His one talon had broken off but no vessel fluid leaked. He stuck it back in his mouth.

"Kartok," he mumbled around it. "Good. Keep going."

She and her brother continued their work, he at shredding the bed and she at rattling the frame. Geluven tore past the layer of springs.

"I think I've only got to rip the top barrier to reach him."

He pushed his arm through the opening he'd created and dug around. The boy choked out another cry.

"MOM!"

A door opened somewhere on the other side of the house and a female voice called out.

"Okay, Ethan. I'm coming. Mommy's coming."

"I've almost got him," Geluven said.

"Here, let me help you."

Antora reached an arm into the hole. Even though her claws were diminutive by Pravusian standards, she and Geluven just might get their prize sooner with her help.

As Antora pushed against the top layer, feeling the soft meaty quality of the boy beyond the thin fabric, the door of the bedroom opened to her right. She nudged her brother. After extracting themselves from the mattress they ceased all movement.

"Ethan," the boy's mother spoke. "I'm here. Are you all right?"

"Mommy, mommy. There are monsters under my bed."

Antora looked at her brother and put a finger to her slats. He held his hands still, inches below the shredded boxed spring. The siblings locked eyes as they listened to the exchange above them.

"Ethan, did you have a nightmare?"

"No, there are monsters under my bed."

"Sweetie, there are no such things as monsters."

"But I heard them. They moved the bed!"

"Ethan," the mother said, sounding weary and frustrated.

"Just look, Mom. Please?"

"Aren't you getting a little old for this?"

"Please, just look."

She sighed and her weight shifted off the bed. Antora grabbed her brother's hand then turned her head to watch the woman's feet shuffle back as she bent her knees. Bracing her hands on the floor for support, the woman lowered her body.

Antora noticed the human's nails were stained a dark crimson. They didn't eat children, too, did they?

Before Antora could ponder the question further, the human mother lowered her face to look underneath the bed. She stared directly at Antora, but, as she and the rest of the Pravusi world already knew, the adult human couldn't see either her or her brother. The two remained motionless though. There was no proof that the adults couldn't detect movement and the pair didn't want to take any chances.

"Ethan, I don't see anything."

"They're right there. I know it."

The mother scanned the entire area underneath the bed but still didn't see Antora or Geluven. Sighing, the woman stood then sat on the bed. The springs squeaked under her weight.

"Sweetie, I promise, there are no monsters under your bed."

"But Mom, I..."

"Enough, Ethan. I looked under the bed and I didn't see any monsters."

"But,"

"Ethan, you know I wouldn't lie to you, right?"

"I guess."

"And I'd never let anything bad happen to you."

"Yeah, I know."

"So you believe me when I say there are no monsters under your bed? That there are no such things as monsters?"

"Yes, Mommy. I believe you."

The child sounded relieved, as if he truly did believe the parental unit, as if everything Antora and Geluven had done never happened. Her thoughts were confirmed when the mother said good night and left the boy's room.

Once she was gone, Geluven reached for the mattress again but Antora stopped him.

"Wait."

She listened to the footsteps in the hall fade as they moved further away. A door opened and closed then all was quiet. Antora nodded at Geluven.

"All right. Should be safe now."

Geluven continued shredding the mattress with great speed.

"Almost there," he said.

Antora could hear the boy whisper a continuous mantra tainted with fear and desperation.

"There's no such thing as monsters. There's no such thing as monsters.There's no such thing—"

The boy stopped his mumbling just as Geluven shouted his success.

"I'm through!"

Antora could feel the drool moisten her tongue at her brother's exclamation. She reached her hand through the shredded bedding and grabbed a handful of the boy—a leg by the feel of it. The child screamed one last time.

"MOMMY!"

Antora and Geluven shared a smile then pulled the human down through the bed, coverings and all. While Antora enveloped the boy in her arms, securing his struggles and quieting his screams, Geluven opened a portal back to the Underland.

"...top story of the evening. An alert is in effect for the entire tri-county area. Eight year old Ethan James Carson went missing from his Westinville home last night sometime after nine o'clock. He has blond hair, brown eyes, and was last seen wearing a pair of dark blue Spiderman pajamas. Police are scouring the area for Ethan's whereabouts. Investigators aren't sharing details but sources tell us there was no evidence of a break-in, though the boy's room did show signs of a struggle.

"While Mr. and Mrs. Carson haven't been ruled out as suspects in Ethan's disappearance, police are concentrating on the family's relationships with friends, neighbors, and coworkers. Mrs. Carson's ex-husband, and Ethan's biological father, has been named a 'person of interest.'

"If you have any information on this developing story, call the number at the bottom of your screen or contact the Westinville police. Let's all do our part to get Ethan home safe and sound."

Nathaniel skipped down the street jingling the coins in his pocket. His mother had given him 10 cents to spend at the candy store. He'd been particularly well behaved today, she said, and deserved a treat. He pulled his grandfather's watch from his pocket and noted the time. He only had an hour to horse around before he had to be back home. As he made his way down the main thoroughfare he slowed to a walk so he could study the carriage factory.

He loved to sneak into the factory and watch them make carriage after carriage. The process fascinated him. There was a corridor that ran underground between the factory of Caleb's Carriages and its huge warehouse. Nathaniel always managed to sneak in the back door of the warehouse and quietly scurry down to the underground passageway unseen.

Today would be no exception. He made his way around to the back of the warehouse. He could hear the men grunting with the strain of moving cords of wood to the factory line. Kneeling behind a stack of wood panels,

Nathaniel peeked around its edge to see if the coast was clear. No one was near the entrance to the corridor and it was just a few feet away. He dashed to the door and quickly slipped behind it and down into the underground hallway.

At the bottom of a small flight of steps was another door that led into the hallway itself. Nathaniel pushed his way through and closed the door quietly behind him. The corridor stretched out in front of him for 50 feet, jogged to the right, continuing on again for another 50 feet where another door opened up on a flight of stairs that led into the factory.

Along the wall to his right were several doors spaced about 15 feet apart.

They each opened into a small closet or storage space. He could explore down here for hours, poking through each space that was crammed with wood, tools, machine parts, and the occasional mouse.

Today Nathaniel walked down to the second door and slipped into the storage space. In here there were piles of cogs and wheels, drills, scraps of wood, belts and pulleys, chains, saws, and countless other used tools. He pulled the door closed behind him and set his eyes on an old hand drill and some wood scraps.

With the door closed the room became warm rather quickly. Nathanial soon grew tired and fell asleep. Several hours later he awoke, sweating and dizzy. He dreamt of being in a furnace, surrounded by heat and flames, trapped and unable to escape. When his head finally cleared he realized the room was extremely warm and he was sweating profusely. He reached for the doorknob and his hand sizzled on the hot metal. He pulled his hand back and screamed in pain and fear.

Scared now, he blew on his injured hand and wrapped

his other in his shirttail. As soon as he managed to turn the knob, the door blew inward, sending Nathaniel sprawling on his back against the far wall. Bruised but not seriously injured, he looked up. Fire licked along the doorjamb and ceiling. The brick wall directly opposite the storage room, however, was not engulfed in flames. Maybe if he managed to jump through the doorway and press himself against the brick wall, he might be able to escape the fire.

Mustering up all his eight-year old courage, he took a running jump at the doorway and sailed through the flames without incident. Moving quickly to avoid the parts of the floor that were burning, he hopped and jumped until he reached the door at the bottom of the warehouse steps. He tentatively tried the knob. It was warm but not scalding – yet.

He turned and pushed but the door would not budge. He couldn't understand why they would lock it. Pushing and straining, he kept trying to open the door. With each effort, he sobbed and cried until he went mad with fear and began pounding on the door, screaming for help knowing in his heart no one would hear him.

He knew all the men up there had gotten to safety and were clear of the burning building. They wouldn't be listening for a little boy in the underground corridor even if they could hear him over the roar of the flames. He stopped pushing on the door and inched his way back down the brick wall. He made it as far as the first storage room when part of the ceiling above caved in and crashed through the floor in front of him.

Nathaniel jumped back, barely escaping being crushed by the falling debris. He was now trapped in the corner between the pile of burning debris and the locked doorway to the warehouse. The smoke started to pour over him and he coughed violently. He huddled down, pushing himself as far against the wall as he could, and cried softly.

The black smoke blocked out all the light and he could barely see his hand in front of his face. He wanted to go home now. He didn't want to be here by himself in the dark. He didn't want to die alone in the underground corridor. He wanted his mother.

"God damn it, Randy. Do you think you could keep a steady beat sometime today?"

Bronin jabbed the neck of his bass guitar at the drummer for emphasis.

Randy flipped him off.

"You're the one that's hung-over, Bronin. Are you sure you're not the fuck-up today?"

Bronin paused and smiled sheepishly. "Oh, yeah."

As the rhythm section of the rock group, Tripping Foul, had a good guffaw, Carl and Will, the guitarist and singer respectively, rolled their eyes. Will tapped the microphone.

"Uh, hello? When you two ladies are finished, we need to get back to rehearsal."

Bronin whined. "But, Will, we've been here for three hours already. I think my hand has gone numb."

"And if you were alone in your bedroom right now, I'd believe it," retorted Will. "But you're not. We've only got a month before the next gig. We've got to practice."

Carl slowly removed his guitar from over his shoulder. "Bronin's right, Will. I know you just want us to be prepared but we've been here all morning. Another five minutes or five hours won't do us any good today. Let's pack it up."

Will sighed. They were right. And even if they weren't, it was three against one. He clicked the power off on his microphone and wrapped up the cords and stand. He locked up his own guitar as the rest of the group packed up their gear for the day. Over the next half-hour they hauled most of their equipment from the rehearsal space to their cars.

Will waved the other three off as he ran back into the building, realizing he left his coat inside. He jogged down a small flight of steps and through a narrow door which opened onto 50-foot long hallway. It angled to the right and continued forward for another 50 feet. The far end of the hall ended in another doorway, which led to another small flight of steps. Those steps led to the first floor lobby of the building above them.

There were several small rooms to his right and the second one was the band's rehearsal space. Will quickly recovered his jacket from the corner of the room. As he turned to leave, the door slammed shut. Frowning, he walked over to the door and tried the knob. Locked.

"Ha, ha, guys. Very funny. Open the door."

He leaned his ear against the door but heard nothing. A sudden wave of exhaustion washed over him. He tried the knob one more time but became too tired to really care if it opened or not. He slumped down onto the nearest chair and promptly fell asleep.

Will gasped and his eyes flew open. At first he didn't realize where he was. As consciousness crawled upon him, he recognized the practice space. Rubbing his eyes, he stood and wiped the sweat from his brow. Sweat? Was the practice space always this warm and he had just never noticed before?

Frowning, he grabbed the doorknob and jumped back

in pain. It was scorching hot. His hand was already blistering. With his uninjured hand he felt the wood of the door. It was hot. Wincing, he wrapped his jacket around his good hand and pried open the door. He quickly shielded his face, expecting a blast of heat from the fire that must be raging in the hallway.

Nothing. There were no flames, no heat, nothing. Carefully, Will poked his head out the door and looked up and down the corridor. The air was a little stuffy but nothing to indicate a fire burning anywhere nearby. He looked down at his burnt palm. Shivering with fear, he ran to the end of the hallway, threw open the door, dashed up the steps, and burst out into the alleyway behind the building.

Randy, Bronin, and Carl were still standing by their cars and talking. The all turned to stare at Will as he raced over to them. Pale faced and shaking, Will told them what happened. Randy and Bronin looked at each other and then burst into laughter.

"Nice try, Will. That was your best story yet," Randy joked as he nudged Will in his ribs.

"He's just trying to get us back in there and then trap us into practicing some more. Get over it, Will. We're done for the day, ok?"

As Randy and Bronin joked, Carl looked down at Will's hand and frowned.

Several blisters were ballooning with fluid already. He pointed to it while jabbing Randy in the shoulder.

"How do you explain that?"

Randy stopped laughing. He grabbed Will's hand and pulled it up to his face for a closer inspection.

"Shit, Will. What did you do to yourself?"

"What did I...? Oh just forget it."

Exasperated, Will stalked off to his own car. Bronin and Randy shrugged in unison and slowly walked back to their vehicles.

"I hope this doesn't fuck up his playing," Bronin muttered.

As the bassist and drummer drove off, Carl waved absently to them. He made pretense of arranging his equipment in the trunk so Bronin and Randy wouldn't see him staring off in the direction Will drove. He's known Will long enough to know when he was shoveling manure and when he wasn't. Whatever had taken place, Carl could see that Will was honestly scared.

Something about Will's story nudged a small block of memory in Carl's brain. He'd heard a story like it before but he just couldn't remember where or when. Maybe he'd look into it over the weekend.

The following week they met again for another rehearsal. Will's hand was, miraculously, almost healed. There were only faint wrinkles and slight circular scars where the blisters had formed but even those were fading. Randy and Bronin ribbed him for pulling a fast one on them but Carl was silent. Will grumbled something about assholes anonymous and warmed up his guitar.

Afterwards, as everyone was packing up, Bronin stayed plugged in. He wanted to stay a little longer to work on the new songs. He kept tripping up during the chorus and speeding through the last few measures. Will mumbled a 'whatever' under his breath and raced out the door. He still seemed spooked from last week and wanted nothing more than to get the hell out of the rehearsal space. Randy and

Bronin joked about it some more but Carl interrupted them.

"Don't you think it's strange, what happened to Will? I thought I'd heard about something similar happening years ago but I couldn't remember the details. So I was doing some research on the history of this city over the weekend. Pontiac had a huge fire downtown in 1840. 25 buildings were destroyed."

Bronin and Randy exchanged looks. "So?" they questioned in unison.

"So," continued Carl, "this entire block was destroyed. This building used to be a carriage factory. The corridor linked the Caleb family carriage factory to its warehouse. The brick out in the hallway is from the original structure. The factory, which was the building over us and to the north, was rebuilt. But the warehouse wasn't. That's why the corridor opens into an alleyway on one end and a building on the other."

Randy raised an eyebrow. "Again I say, so?"

"Well, don't you think it's odd that Will thought there was a fire here, burned his hand on the doorknob, only to discover nothing was amiss?"

Bronin looked at Randy. "Amiss? Did he just say, 'amiss'?"

Randy held up his hands. "What are you saying, Carl? That Will had a run-in with a ghost fire from 1840?"

"Well, yeah, I guess."

"Carl, I think it's time you took up drinking."

"Randy, I'm serious."

"I can see that. That's why I suggest a diet heavy in depressants. Bronin, see ya later."

Randy grabbed his stick bag and headed down the hall. Carl looked to Bronin, who held up his hands, signifying the 'don't even start with me' gesture. Sighing, Carl grabbed his guitar and jogged after Randy. He caught up to him in the alleyway.

"Randy, wait a minute."

"Carl, if you've come to say good night, then I bid you the same. But if you've chased after me with more of this post-modern ghost story shit..."

"All I'm saying is something happened to Will. I don't know what exactly but I think it's worth investigating. You've got an uncle that works in the Hall of Records for Pontiac, right? Can't you ask him to do a little digging?"

"Have him dig into the records to find info on the 1840 fire because we think it came into the future and attacked our friend?"

"I don't know. Tell him you heard a story about the fire and were curious. Tell him you've heard ghost stories from the locals. Tell him anything. Just see what you can find out, please?"

Randy shook his head. Carl would do anything for his friends but right now he was creeping Randy out. He was Carl's friend, however, so he'd humor him. Besides, Carl's ideas were giving him the willies so if for no other reason, at least Randy could quell his own apprehension.

As Carl sped out of the parking lot and Randy headed for City Hall, Bronin stayed back at the rehearsal space and continued to practice. His fingers flew up and down the neck of his bass as he tapped out a complicated rhythm with his feet. He stumbled over a long set of sixteenth notes and came in late for the refrain. Cursing, he wiped the sweat from his forehead and began again.

Approaching the same set of notes he furrowed his brow in concentration. Drops of sweat rolled into his eyes, the salt stinging them and blurring his vision. Frustrated, he pulled the bass over his head and rested it on the stand behind him. He grabbed the front of his shirt and wiped his face dry.

As he stared at his soaked shirt, wondering why it was so damned hot in the rehearsal space, he smelled something burning. He whipped his head around to look at his amp. It hummed quietly in the corner as it always did. He checked Will's and Carl's amps but they were off. He looked at the closed door and saw smoke curling underneath from the hallway.

Panicked, he ran to the door and laid his hand on the wood. It was warm. He touched the doorknob with a finger to test it and quickly pulled it back. The metal was scorching. He grabbed an end of his shirt, wrapped it around his hand, and twisted the knob carefully. Suddenly the door blew inward and he was thrown to the back of the room.

Stunned, a little bruised but unharmed, Bronin shook his head to clear it. He looked up. Bright orange flames licked the doorjamb but the hallway floor and brick wall looked untouched—for now. He had to get the hell out of there before the smoke and flames overtook him. Maybe if he ran for the door he could jump through it and get to the brick wall unscathed.

Taking a deep breath, Bronin ran at the door. Just as he leapt through the opening he saw a young boy pressed against the brick. He was feeling his way along the wall towards the doorway to the alley down the hall. He was dressed in wool knickers and a soot-covered dress shirt. His short blonde hair was ruffled with sweat.

Just before Bronin reached the wall, the boy turned. He screamed and covered his face with his arms as if they alone could protect his mind from the horrifying visage of the boy.

He reached for Bronin, crying and whispering, and they both disappeared into the wall, leaving behind only a dark wet smudge on the crumbling bricks.

———

Randy drove his car into the parking lot of Pontiac's City Hall building. He walked up the entrance steps, shaking his head, hardly believing he was doing this. After passing through security he headed for his uncle's office on the second floor.

He knocked on the door marked "Historical Records" and was answered with a gruff "What?" from within. Grinning, Randy pushed open the door.

"Now is that anyway to speak to family, Uncle Dave?"

Without looking up from his paperwork, he responded, "It's the only way."

Randy took a seat opposite his uncle's desk. He waited patiently until his uncle was ready for him. Scribbling out his signature for authorization on an order for a new filing cabinet, Randy's uncle finished with the form and looked up at his nephew, smiling.

"Now, as I was saying. What?"

Embarrassed, Randy looked at the floor. "I, uh. Well, I was wondering, um, that is, do you know..."

"For crying out loud, boy. What do you want? I'm up to my left nut in paperwork. I haven't got all day."

Randy sighed. "What do you know about the history of Pontiac?"

His uncle gaped at him. "Exactly where do you think I work, son? Circuit City?"

"What I mean is, do you know anything about the big fire here back in 1840?"

He frowned. "Of course. Why?"

"What can you tell me about it?"

"You mean besides things being on fire?"

"C'mon, Uncle Dave. I'm serious."

"Well, most of the main thoroughfare was destroyed. Twenty-five buildings in all. As a matter of fact, the building where you and your buddies practice in was built on the original foundation of the old Caleb carriage factory. Shame, really."

A tickle of fear crept up the nape of Randy's neck making the small hairs stand on end. "What do you mean?"

"Well, all the factory workers were able to get out before the building was destroyed by the fire. But part of the warehouse collapsed, blocking an entryway into the underground corridor that connected it to the main factory. Apparently, a young boy, a local merchant's son, was playing down there and got trapped. He died in the fire."

"Holy shit."

"Yep. They found him two days later in the corridor by the door that had been blocked by the ruins of the warehouse. More than likely he tried to get out that way but, obviously, he didn't make it."

"Holy shit."

"Uh, yeah. Apparently part of the corridor's ceiling caved in, trapping him in the corner near the warehouse door. The bricks of the wall he leaned against basically became super-heated and... Well, let's just say that all that was left of the kid was pretty much a blackened skeleton."

Randy frowned. "Did the ever find out who the boy was?"

Uncle Dave scratched his head. "I believe so. His name was Nathaniel Brown. I remember reading something about the kid having his grandfather's pocket watch on him that day. For some reason, it wasn't completely destroyed by the heat. Maybe Nathaniel's body somehow protected it. There were only a few scratches on it and the monogram on the inside was untouched, which gave them proof beyond any doubt that it was Nathaniel. Sad that a little trinket of machinery survived but not the boy, huh?"

Randy stood slowly. He quietly thanked his uncle for his help and promised to call him later in the week. He left the office, gently closing the door behind him. He could still hear his uncle asking him if he was okay but he couldn't answer.

He walked away in a daze. He was only a few feet from his uncle's office when a hand on his arm stopped him. He jumped and looked up to see the custodian, Tom Dyer, frowning in concern at him. Tom was a tall wiry man in his mid-forties whose bright grey eyes matched his city overalls. Normally Randy liked to stop and chat with the janitor but today he just wanted to get out of this building.

"You okay, Randy?"

"Uh, yeah, Tom. I'm fine."

"Hey, I couldn't help but overhear what you and your uncle were talking about. You know, he didn't tell you everything."

Randy's face pinched in confusion. "What do you mean?"

"That building where the old carriage factory used to be? There's a corridor that runs underneath it and..."

"Yeah, Tom, I know. My friends and I rent a rehearsal space down there."

Tom's face blanched. He grabbed Randy's arm and squeezed with a strength that belied his scarecrow build. The panic in his voice was mirrored in his pinched features.

"It's not safe. Things happen, people get hurt. You boys have got to get out of there!"

Randy's face froze as the tingle of fear at the nape of his neck transformed into an icy hand that gripped his spinal cord and gave it a good jerk. Will's story. His hand. Uncle Dave's info on Nathaniel. Randy had stopped listening to Tom's rambling and tried to free himself from the rambling janitor's death grip. But suddenly the man's words stopped him.

"Wait, Tom. What was that you said?"

"I said some people claim to feel the heat from the fire when they're in there. Some people say they can smell smoke or see the fire itself. Of course, those are the people that lived to tell their tales."

Randy couldn't speak. He couldn't believe what he was hearing. Tom continued.

"You see, my great-great-grandfather was just a boy when the fire hit. He lived, of course, and he passed down stories through my family about how once they rebuilt the carriage factory, people started seeing things. Then they started disappearing."

"Why haven't I heard about any of this before?"

Tom smirked. "Because them bigwigs in real estate wouldn't be making no money if they told people looking to rent their property that there was a ghost running around their building, let alone one that kills 'em."

"Wait, wait. Do they see the fire or do they see ghosts?"

"Well, I suppose the fire is kinda like a ghost itself. It has appeared to people without the boy."

Randy gulped. "Do you mean Nathaniel?"

"Yep. Of course, I've only heard of one person who's seen the boy and lived to tell the tale. He's up in Northville in that loony bin. Mostly he just mumbles and drools as he bounces off them rubber walls. But every now and again the staff says he'll hunker down in a corner, grabbin' at the air and yellin' out Nathaniel's name."

"How do you know all this?"

Tom looked down at his shoes and kicked at the broom he was holding. "Because it's my brother in that nuthouse."

He looked up at Randy, his eyes wide with fear. "You boys get outta that place. It's not safe. It's not..."

Randy's own eyes mirrored Tom's horror but not from the story. He just remembered that Bronin stayed after rehearsal today to practice—alone. He thanked Tom absently as he pulled out his cell phone and dialed Bronin's number. No answer.

"Damn it!" Randy cursed under his breath. He ran for his car and dialed Carl's number. He picked up on the second ring.

"Carl? It's Randy. I think Bronin's in trouble. Meet me over at the rehearsal space. See if you can get a hold of Will, too. "

"Randy, what's going...?"

"Just do it, Carl. I found out a little info on our phantom fire. Turns out the fire isn't our only ghost. There's something else. Meet me over there!"

He punched the 'end' button and hopped into his car. He just hoped Carl, Will, and he could get to Bronin in time. As he pulled into the parking lot of the old building, Carl screeched around the corner and parked beside him. Randy frowned, confused as to how Carl got there so quickly.

"I stopped at the deli down the street for a quick bite. I was halfway through when you called. I got Will on the phone but he hung up before I could ask him to come back up here. What's going on?"

Randy filled him in on the back-story to the fire and the ghost. After explaining how Nathaniel died, Carl's face fell. He raced for the back door in the alley that led down to the corridor. Bursting through, he screamed for Bronin.

When no one answered he rushed for the practice room door.

Randy raced behind him and they both rushed into the rehearsal space, empty, save for Bronin's bass and amp which were both still powered up. The quiet hum from the amplifier added a spooky undertone to the whole scene that made Randy's skin vibrate with fear. Carl bolted from the room and ran down to the other end of the hallway, yelling out Bronin's name.

Randy stood staring at the lonely bass guitar, rubbing a hand over his sweat-dampened face. As soon as he realized how badly he was perspiring, Will's story sprang to the front of his mind. He quickly sidestepped out of the rehearsal space before the door had a chance to slam shut.

Smoke quietly began to curl around Randy's feet. The hallway felt like an oven and sweat dripped into his eyes. He dabbed at his face with his shirtsleeve. Randy could hear a soft whimpering coming from down the hall, near the door to the alleyway. He fanned the smoke away as it climbed up towards his face and he squinted at the end of the hall. He could barely make out a lone shape huddled in the corner.

"Hello? Nathaniel, is that you?"

As he neared the end of the hallway, Randy could hear the distinct sobbing and hitching gasps of a crying child. He waved his arms wildly to try and clear the black smoke that had now engulfed him. Somewhere behind him he could hear Carl calling his name. But he couldn't give up his search for Nathaniel.

Suddenly, two pale arms reached up to him from the dark corner. The boy's quiet whisper floated up to Randy's ears. The lonely pleading in Nathaniel's voice was deafening.

"Help me. I don't want to be here all by myself. Please stay with me."

Nathaniel grabbed Randy's hands and pulled. Despite the cold fear lodged in his throat, Randy could only drop down to the floor as the boy guided him. As he pushed himself up against the brick wall he could feel the boy sidle up against him, still clutching Randy's hands in his own small grasp. The boy's blonde hair was dirty with soot from the fire and black smudges colored Nathaniel's cheeks.

"Randy! Randy!"

Carl was standing near the practice room door when he saw Randy hunker down in the smoke-filled corner. He could just make out the shape of a small child sitting next to him, clinging to Randy as if he could save him from the fire. He had to get Randy away from Nathaniel before it was too late.

He ran down the hall, waving his arms and screaming Randy's name.

He looked at Carl and held up a hand to warn him off. He wrapped his arm protectively around the boy. As Carl got closer to them Randy could feel Nathaniel tense beside him. Randy shouted to Carl.

"Carl! Stop where you are. Don't come any closer."

Confused, Carl stopped in the middle of the hallway just as the ceiling caved in front of him. He jumped back a few steps and waved away the dust from the debris. Coughing, he tried to call to Randy.

"Randy, what...?"

"Carl, please. Just leave. It's okay."

"But..."

"Carl! Get out! Now!"

Carl gagged as more black smoke rolled around him. The more he tried to wave it away the thicker it appeared. Angry and scared, he did the only thing he could. He backed away and headed for the exit at the opposite end of the corridor. Randy watched him disappear into the blackness then relaxed, knowing Carl would be safe.

Randy cried as he rocked the boy back and forth in his arms. In order to end the cycle of hauntings, Randy realized he couldn't leave him alone here anymore. He had to give Nathaniel what he most desperately needed. At least no one else would get hurt now.

Suddenly all the smoke whooshed away as if a strong wind blew through the corridor. Randy looked down at the boy and tried to hide his fear. Nathaniel lipless mouth stretched open as he grinned. His blackened skin was pulled taught over his tiny skull. It had split along his cheek when he smiled. Viscous crimson blood oozed along his jaw slowly dripping off his chin and onto Randy's jeans.

Randy grimaced and smoothed down the few remaining tufts of hair sticking up on the boy's head. Even though Nathaniel's eyes burned out years ago, Randy could still see the soulful expression hidden in the empty sockets—one of longing and sadness.

"Don't worry. I'll stay with you. You'll never be alone again."

Nathaniel giggled with the innocence of a child not charred by death's fiery hand and wrapped his skeletal arms tightly around Randy's waist. The light of the living world faded and slowly the corridor disappeared. As tears slipped down Randy's cheeks, he tried to console the boy with a gentle squeeze. Nathaniel breathed a sigh of release and contentment. And as darkness enveloped them, Randy breathed with him.

TOO SOON

She stood at the edge of the water, her toes tickled by small briny kisses from the Gulf. The sun beat down on her pink floral-patterned blouse, warming her old bones. Her permanent- styled white hair ruffled in a stiff breeze off the water.

Her left hand, holding her crossword booklet, pulled up to her chest in a reflex as a young man, clad in nothing but one of those European swim suits, passed by. He nodded and smiled.

"Hello."

"Good morning," she replied.

As he moved away, she tsk-ed under her breath. In her day, men didn't present themselves in such a vulgar manner. It wasn't necessary to put their privates on such a public display. Her Harvey never dressed like that.

Harvey was a Marine during the Korean War. She met him at a Welcome Home dinner dance the local USO chapter had organized for all the returning soldiers in her neighborhood. He had asked her to dance minutes after she'd arrived. She was hopelessly in love seconds after that.

They had celebrated their fifty-third wedding anniversary last month. It turned out they weren't as compatible as they would have liked, but divorce in those days was taboo so they stayed together.

They did see many happy days in their marriage, though: Harvey's hip replacement, his mother's death, and the surprise party she threw for him that caused his first heart attack. Maybe she just enjoyed those experiences. There were times, she knew, when only Harvey felt happy. The memory that sprang to her mind involved a large pile of gravy drenched mashed potatoes, a rusty bolt, and an emergency trip to the dentist to get her dentures fixed.

One thing she knew for certain was they both loved to take their yearly vacation down to Siesta Key, Florida. They'd honeymooned on its white sandy beaches and returned every year since.

She stared out at the crystalline water, the sun dappling its diamonds for anyone willing to bear witness. She remembered how she and Harvey had made love under the cabana on their fifth anniversary. He'd tried to drown her in the hotel pool on their fifteenth. And she gave him his second heart attack on their fortieth.

Those were good times. Now that he was gone, it didn't seem quite the same here.

The beach, stretching north to the end of the key and south to the Point, appeared longer than she remembered. The Gulf sat menacing to the west, far larger, deeper, and more dangerous than when she and Harvey used to watch the sunsets. The pelicans, gulls, terns, and even the sand pipers reminded her of the movie, *The Birds*, and they flocked closer to her, circling as if they knew she was alone now. Did she just hear the clicking of a sand crab's claws?

She turned to face each of the cardinal directions,

seeking the next threat. Her heart pounded with a fear she'd never known before—the fear of being alone. Her gaze settled on the dark expanse of water. In all her eighty three years, she never regretted any choice she'd ever made. Until today.

She regretted not putting the cyanide in her own breakfast as well.

J oe loved the holidays. He enjoyed putting up the icicle lights along the gutters of his house, setting up a big fat Santa Claus, along with a sleigh and full reindeer company, on the roof. The best part of the winter holiday, though, was competing with Bob Jones.

Bob lived across the street and over the past ten years, he and Joe built up their Christmas displays from the simple foam candy canes lining their walkways to the monster light show it had become today. Along with the candy canes, Joe had thousands of lights, choirs of lighted plastic angels, four statues of carolers with homemade outfits his wife, Kathleen, fashioned for them, and several spotlights pointed at the house—red, green, and yellow, and one that shone "Season's Greetings" against the garage.

Additionally, Bob had twenty presents around the evergreen tree in his front yard, each wrapped in a vast spectrum of colors and textures, and a huge teddy bear adorned with a great red ribbon tied in a bow. Electric candles burned in every window and fake snow adorned his front door. But this year, the truly spectacular feature was a brilliant light over his house, a free-floating phenomenon with a beauty that Joe envied.

One night Joe walked across the street and banged on Bob's door.

Answering it with a hot mug of apple cider in one hand and a plain donut in the other, Bob grinned around a mouthful of the doughy morsel and spit some of it out in greeting to Joe.

"Hey, Joe. Waddya know?"

"Don't 'waddya know' me, Bob. What is it?"

Bob frowned.

"What's what?"

"You know exactly what. That light floating over your house." Bob grinned again and walked out on the porch.

"Oh, yeah. Beautiful, ain't she?"

"Sure but what is it?"

"Remember I told you my mother passed away a couple of months ago?"

"Yeah."

Bob jerked a thumb over his shoulder.

"Well, that's her."

"What do you mean, 'that's her?'"

"I mean that light is her. Her spirit, if you will. I was talking to her the other day, well more to myself really, when this light appeared before me. It spoke in her voice and knew so many personal things that it couldn't have been a hoax."

Joe stared at his neighbor for several long minutes. Finally, he spoke. "You're so full of it, Bob. If you don't want to tell me what it is, then fine but don't make up this crap."

"I'm not lying. I'll prove it." He turned to the floating light.

"Mom? Can you come here for a minute? Joe doesn't believe you're real." The light flared red and zoomed down toward Joe. He backed up, stammering out a retraction.

"I, I didn't say you weren't real. It's just that I find it difficult to believe that you're—"

A high-pitched scruffy voice that sounded just like Bob's mother spoke but whether it was aloud or in his head, Joe couldn't tell.

"Joe Smith, are you calling my son a liar? Some things never change. Do you remember four years ago, when you told your wife that Bob gambled away two hundred dollars you said you loaned him, without asking her I might add, when it was actually you who lost it at the track?"

"How did you know that?"

The light cackled like an old woman. "I'm dead. I know everything."

Joe looked back to Bob.

"I'm sorry I didn't believe you. This really is your mom, isn't it?"

"You bet. She decided to help me with my holiday display here. Isn't she doing a fabulous job?"

The sphere glided up over Bob's house and increased its brilliance to brighten up the entire yard. Suddenly the spotlights at Joe's house sparked, fizzed, and went out. Joe could hear the smile in Bob's voice.

"Aw, that's a shame, Joe. Your house doesn't quite look the same without those lights, does it?"

Joe turned back to reply. Bob stood over him, frowning and holding the steaming cider an inch from Joe's left eye.

"Better go check the wires. You don't want a short to cause a fire or anything, do you?"

Joe backed away into the street. Bob grinned again and went back inside.

The light danced back and forth as if laughing. Joe frowned and went to look at the cords from the spotlights. Each was intact as were the outlets. For some reason, the lights had just stopped working.

He turned to look at Bob's house. The orb still danced its happy little jig. Joe realized that she was responsible for shorting out the lights. The old bat never had liked him. He ripped out the plugs from each of the outlets, cursing Bob and his mother.

He dragged the spotlights into his garage and sat down at his workbench, defeated. How could he compete with a ghost? If only his father were here. Joe's dad passed away last year and it had been hard for him to cope. He never talked to him though, like Bob did with his mother, because he felt ridiculous and feared people would think he was crazy.

He glanced around the garage, then pulled off his hat, crumpling it between his hands. He looked up at the ceiling.

"Dad? I never really believed in the whole life-after-death thing but I've seen something fantastic tonight. I'm hoping it wasn't a joke or a hallucination. I'm hoping it was real because I need your help, dad. Dad?"

When nothing happened after five minutes, Joe chided himself for being a fool. He crammed the hat back on his head, his face burning in embarrassment, and headed for the side door of the garage. As he reached for the knob, a spark of electricity burst between his fingers. Jumping back he noticed the garage seemed brighter than before. Slowly he turned around and a white orb floated before him.

"Who are you?"

"I think you already know the answer to that, son."

"Dad?"

"Of course it's me. You were just asking for me, weren't you?"

"Well, yeah, but I never thought... Oh, dad, I'm so glad you're here."

"I know, son. I know what's going on with you and Bob. I also know that crab of an old lady he calls his mother is helping him. So I'm going to give you a hand, so to speak."

Joe frowned.

"How do I know it's really you?"

The swirling light bobbed in close to Joe's face and he felt a sudden sharp pain across the bridge of his nose. His father used to *thwap* two fingers there when Joe was younger to discourage him from crying.

Joe rubbed his nose.

"I'm sorry I doubted you, dad."

"That's all right. Now let's get to work. We've got to come up with something to outdo those damned Joneses for what they pulled tonight."

"Right!" Joe cried. He hesitated at the door. "What can we do?"

"You just leave that to me."

His father bobbed out the side door and shot over the house. As Joe ran up the orb started spinning and weaving around. Suddenly, it shot out streams of light that sparkled, like jets of luminescent crystals. In a matter of minutes, Joe's entire front yard and house were covered in flecks of silver that winked and flashed in the light from his father.

Bob rushed out of his front door. He stood in the street, mouth agape, dumfounded. Even the light from Bob's mother dimmed in the awesome display. Joe's dad spun faster. Small sparks flew out and fell harmlessly to the snow.

Larger ones arced out over the street, straight at Bob Jones. He ducked away from one but a second hit him squarely on the head. As he beat at it and danced around to avoid another collision, Joe's dad slowly moved forward, bringing the shower of sparks closer to Bob's roof. Once they hit it, the roof caught fire.

Bob's mother spun in circles, her color changing from orange to red in a panic. Bob ran for the hose but found an empty spigot instead. He scrambled toward his garage and came stumbling back out, tripping over the uncoiling monster as he ran. The fire was small but spreading quickly. If he didn't act soon enough, his house would be history.

He finally managed to untangle the hose then hooked it up. Bob turned the nozzle and reached for the sprayer attached to the end. When he squeezed, nothing happened. Looking down, he saw a kink in the line. He grabbed the hose on each side and pulled, stretching and straining but the kink didn't budge. He threw the hose down and spun around to face his neighbor.

"Joe, you can't do this! My house, my home!"

"I'm not doing anything, Bob."

Bob's face flushed red with anger. He pulled at his hair and Joe held up his hand.

"Don't have a stroke, Bob. I'll handle this."

He looked up at his father and nodded. The orb flashed green once. Bob frowned and looked at his roof. The fire was still spreading. He turned back to Joe, a question furrowing his brow and Joe pointed at the hose. Bob saw the kink was gone. He grabbed it and shot a stream of water at the fire. Soon it was out but Bob's roof was going to need some repairs unless he wanted it to snow in his living room.

Joe could see the relief wash over Bob as he stared up at his smoldering roof but it was short lived. He tossed the hose to the side and stormed across the street to confront Joe. As he approached, the glowing orb hovered over Joe's left shoulder and Bob faltered. Joe smirked.

"You remember my dad, don't you, Bob? Well, he'll be helping me during the holidays this year. Though you'd like to know. G'night, neighbor."

He turned, then stopped, and spun on his heel to face Bob again. When he did, his voice burned with a warning.

"Oh, yeah. Don't ever threaten me again, understand?" Bob gulped then nodded his head in understanding.

A smile curved Joe's mouth.

"Great. Have a good night...neighbor."

By the following Saturday, Joe's and Bob's competition in decor had turned into a rivalry of destruction. With their parents' help, the two men had managed to break almost every window in each other's homes and blow off both front doors. The strings of lights at Joe's house lay broken and lifeless in his yard, and the teddy bear on Bob's lawn lay decapitated and de-limbed, the head spiked on an evergreen tree.

On Saturday night, Joe rigged a bomb under the dead bushes on the side of Bob's house. He chose them because Sparky, Bob's cocker spaniel, relieved himself on them every night at nine sharp. He glanced at his watch and noted the time–8:50pm. By 8:56, he was done and back across the street in his own home.

Sitting comfortably in his recliner, Joe turned the remote detonator over and over in his hands, tracing circles with his index finger around the red button in the middle.

"Hey, dad. See anything yet?"

"Not yet."

Joe smiled to himself and studied the remote while his father kept watch through the broken remnants of his front window. At nine o'clock, Joe heard the door open across the street as Bob's wife, Sarah, let Sparky out into the yard. She was yelling at Bob to stop this ridiculous feud with Joe or she'd go home to her mother.

"Okay, Joe. Get ready. When I give the signal, you push the button."

Grinning, Joe concentrated on the remote. He could hear Sparky as the dog yipped and barked during his nightly ritual but he wouldn't let that distract him from the task at hand. Suddenly, his father shouted.

"Now, son. NOW!"

Joe pressed the button and cheered when he heard the explosion. He ran to the window, eager to see Bob's reaction. He saw a large form laying in the front yard and frowned. He didn't think Sparky was that big. Then he spotted the dog as it crawled out from beneath the evergreen tree and approached the still form. As Joe shook his head, Bob ran out of his house, screaming in despair. He fell to his knees and cradled his wife's mangled corpse, seeming not to notice as his white sweatshirt turned red with her blood.

As he rocked back and forth, clutching Sarah to his chest, he spotted Joe as he stood in what was left of his picture window.

Bob lay Sarah's body gently on the ground. He stepped around the corpse and crossed the street. His mother swooped down ahead of him for her own fight with Joe's dad. As the two orbs rose above the house, circling each other, Bob stepped onto Joe's front lawn and picked up his pace. By the time he hit Joe's front door, he was running full speed and shrieking. The skirmish was over. It was time to go to war.

Bob threw himself on Joe, pinning him to the floor. He

pummeled him with a fury Joe never knew existed. With two quick strikes, Bob broke Joe's nose with a sickening crunch. He salivated through a wicked grin and pulled his arm back for another blow. When he did Joe double-fisted Bob in the stomach, knocking the wind out of him. As Bob rolled to the side, wheezing for breath, Joe wriggled out from beneath him and ran for the kitchen.

Screaming for his father's help, Joe searched for a weapon. He grabbed an eight-inch stainless steel carving knife from a wooden block on the counter. Joe tried to explain as he walked back to the foyer where Bob knelt, arms folded across his stomach.

"I swear to God, Bob. I didn't mean to hurt her. I didn't mean for Sarah..."

Bob glared as he struggled to stand, his rage stabbing in its coldness. Just then, Kathleen came down the stairs. She was pulling on her robe, her eyes bleary with sleep. Before she could speak, Bob was on his feet and running again. Joe turned quickly and pointed the knife at him.

Bob grabbed Joe's wrist and held it with both hands. He spun them around to face Kathleen. Joe heard his own scream of protest as Bob rushed forward and they both plunged the knife into Kathleen's chest, piercing her heart. Her eyes fluttered in surprise. She looked at Joe and smiled softly. After caressing his cheek with the last ounce of strength she owned, Kathleen slumped to the floor, dead.

Joe released his grip on the knife then fell to his knees, sobbing and trying to shake her back to life. Helpless to save her, he leaned over to kiss her forehead and whisper goodbye. He stood, walked slowly over to the sink, and grabbed the rolling pin on the drying rack. He turned to face Bob, raised the rolling pin above his head, and screamed.

Bob ran for the door. Just as he went through it, Joe caught up with him and smashed the rolling pin against the back of his head. Bob stumbled and fell down the porch steps and rolled into the front yard. He lay on his back, stunned, a warm pool of blood spreading beneath him, melting the snow.

Joe knelt beside him. He raised the rolling pin one more time, hoping to crush Bob's face into his brain. As he bent forward for the final blow, Bob raised the carving knife. He had no strength but it wasn't needed. Joe rushed himself upon the blade, where it lodged into his heart and he collapsed on top of Bob. Each of their final moments was spent staring into the other's eyes as their lives ebbed away.

The orbs floated down and hovered over the two dead men. One blinked and took the shape of a man in his thirties, dressed in a conservative suit circa 1924. The other took the form of a sixty-five year old woman in a shimmery gold silk dress. The two looked at each other and guffawed with delight.

"Well done, mother. This was even better than last year."

"We make a good team, just as we did when we were alive. I wasn't about to let Death spoil all our fun."

"Exactly," the male ghost replied. "Just because we've been damned to roam the earth for all eternity doesn't mean we can't enjoy ourselves, now does it?"

"And I thought killing when we were alive was fun. But we have so much more freedom in this form, don't you agree, son?"

He nodded.

"These pitiful creatures will believe anything you tell them."

The both laughed and floated down the street. The son pointed at the next block.

"You know, there are a few Jewish families living on the next block and Chanukah is eight days long. Think of the fun we could have with them." The woman chuckled.

"The living are so easy."

DON'T BE A DUMMY

Phil had a bitch of a time getting the duct tape on the dummy. After each crash test, the dummies would sustain more and more damage. To help cut corners, he and the rest of the testing team would secure the loose or broken bits with duct tape so they could get several tests from each dummy before it had to be scrapped.

Some were more resilient than others. He remembered getting four or five tests out of one before it was totally trashed. But its bulky construction probably had something to do with that. Phil was afraid this one was ready for the dumpster after just one run.

"Mitch? Can you give me a hand down here?"

Mitch Parker, the manager on duty today, trotted down the stairs from the main office and leaned into the heap of twisted metal that used to be a four- door sedan. He pushed his forefinger on the dummy's nose and its head listed dangerously to the left. Phil cursed as he tried to wrap more duct tape around its neck.

"Dammit, Mitch. I almost had it fixed. Now are you going to help me or not?"

Before he could answer, the dummy's head rolled off and bounced along the concrete floor. It came to a stop ten feet from the mangled car. Mitch grinned and slapped Phil on the back.

"Sorry, pal. Looks like we need a replacement. Allow me."

Mitch sauntered over to the east wall, picking up the head on the way, tossing it from one hand to the other. He slam-dunked the head in a trash receptacle then danced around in a victory circle as if he had just scored the winning basket in overtime. As he simulated cheering noises from an imaginary crowd, he walked the last few feet to the wall and hit a large red button marked "Replacements".

A spinning red light flashed overhead in time with a buzzer that sounded like an amplified version of Phil's alarm clock. Four men in blue jumpers entered the crash test area through the west wall carrying the replacement dummy, struggling with the heavy load. Mitch whistled as he walked back and stood next to Phil.

"Looks like we got another one from the 'Mountain Man' series. It's about time. They've been sending us so many 'Matchsticks' lately I thought I was never going to have to buy another lighter for my smokes."

Phil stared at his supervisor. He brushed an errant lock of black hair from his eyes. Mitch frowned.

"What's your problem?"

Phil sighed.

"Do you have to do that?"

"Do what?"

Phil pointed to the trashcan. "That!"

Grinning, he pinched Phil's cheek.

"Oh, aren't we the sensitive one? What difference does it make? It can't feel anything, right?"

"That's not the point."

"Then what, oh Morally-High One, is the point?"

"It's just creepy, okay? Besides, what if you damaged it? We'd get a false measurement for the records."

Mitch raised his hands and backed away. "So sorry to have offended your delicate sensibilities, your Ethically-Raised Mightiness. We're not even doing head injury testing today, remember? Strictly torso numbers. Geez, chill out."

He pointed to the new dummy. "Do you want me to help with the replacement or flagellate myself in the corner for my brutish ways?"

Phil nodded as he felt the heat rush to his cheeks. "I'm sorry, man. Sometimes it just gets to me. And yeah, I would appreciate your help with this one."

Mitch grinned. "That's my man. Let's go."

They headed to the control panel near the south wall where a fresh vehicle sat, an oversized pick-up, ready for the next test. The four men had already placed the new dummy in the truck and were walking back to the west exit with the old one. Phil and Mitch positioned the dummy behind the wheel properly, with its hands locked at the ten- and two-o'clock positions on the steering wheel, the right foot on the gas, the left on the floor, and back straight.

Phil looked around, searching. "Hey, where's The Spring?"

The dummies' heads had a tendency to flop forward so the State Crash Testing Institute had manufactured a type of collar that would hold the heads up. It looked like a giant bedspring, hence the nickname. When driving, most people wouldn't be looking down as if there was a tiny circus going on in their pants and they had ringside seats. Without these collars, the crash results would be skewed and the team would be screwed for the whole day.

Mitch patted down the dummy and found The Spring in the front pocket. The SCTI always made sure the dummies were clothed, too. Clothing sometimes got caught on seatbelts, turn signals, or gearshifts, and that created a whole mess of new injuries to be recorded. That's what helped the automotive engineers design safer vehicles. Without this testing work, the Pinto would probably still be a top seller.

After securing the collar on the dummy's neck, Mitch reached for the seatbelt. Before he locked it, he turned to Phil.

"Have we done any tests without the belts today?"

Phil scratched his head. "No, I don't think so."

Mitch let the belt slip back into place. He slapped the dummy on its wide chest.

"Sorry, buddy. But you go without on this ride. See you at the far end." He backed away and Phil shut the door. They both walked behind the control panel and set up the run. The pick-up was set for a 40mph run that would end abruptly at a steel barrier approximately 100 feet away. Without a seatbelt, this could get messy. As the dummy was one of the larger models, though, Phil hoped the steering wheel would keep it from flying through the windshield and give them some good numbers. It would also give them a better chance to reuse this dummy at least one more time before having to scrap it.

Setting the test in motion, Phil and Mitch pulled on their protective goggles. The red light swirled in circles on the ceiling again but a high pitched whistle signaled the beginning of the test. The pick-up jerked forward and soared towards its goal. It folded inward like a paper napkin when it hit the wall. Both Mitch and Phil expected the truck to hold up better than that, but there's just no accounting for shoddy workmanship and cheap materials these days.

As Phil and Mitch approached the crumpled vehicle, it whispered to them with various pings and clicks from all its broken innards. Phil whistled as steam rose from under the hood. Mitch bent down to check under cab and saw a small but growing pool of dark fluid on the running board and concrete floor. He tore off his safety goggles and threw them at the truck.

"Dammit! It's leaking all over the place. And it's gotta be bad because I haven't even opened the door yet. What kind of P-O-S pick-up is this anyway? Shit. Well, we'd better get a good look at the damage before control brings in a replacement."

Mitch grabbed the driver's side door handle and pulled. With the front side panel crumpled, the door only opened an inch. Phil squeezed his hands in the narrow opening and leaned back with all his weight. Between the two of them, the door creaked and groaned as it pushed against the destroyed front end and finally popped open. They weren't quite prepared for the mess they found, especially when the dummy's left arm plopped out onto the floor at their feet.

"Christ on his cross what a mess," Mitch groaned. "If I'd know the damn truck was gonna fold like this, I would've put the frickin' seatbelt on this one. At least it would have reduced the slop a bit, don't you think?"

Mitch nudged Phil in the ribs with his elbow. "Hey, what's wrong with you? You never seen one this bad before?"

Phil felt woozy as he shook his head. He hadn't ever seen one like this.

Granted, he'd only been on the job for six months and always knew, somewhere in the back of his brain, that this would happen sooner or later. He had just hoped it would have been later. Much later.

Mitch grabbed a stainless steel cart and wheeled it over to the truck. He lined the bottom with clear heavy plastic. He picked up the dummy's arm and tossed it into the cart. The ball joint of the humerus stuck out from the torn flesh of the shoulder muscle. Blood oozed onto the plastic sheet and puddled underneath the entire arm, like a marinade on a pork loin. Mitch pulled out a steel ruler from the bottom rack of the cart and measured the angle and depth of the hole the severed arm left on the dummy. Grabbing the clipboard from the rack as well, he noted the measurement on the top sheet.

Phil stood with his mouth hanging open like a rusty mailbox. Mitch nudged him with the clipboard.

"If you're gonna be sick can you please do it in the john? I don't want to have to clean up after you, too."

Mitch continued to poke and prod the dummy for more information. Since it wasn't wearing a seatbelt, the impact threw it into the windshield creating spider web cracks in the glass. Fortunately, the glass held and the dummy had bounced back into the driver's seat. The top half of its face was caved in, the eyes and nose pushed back into the skull. The lower jaw was the only part of the face undamaged so next to the flattened upper portion, the mandible jutted out like the mouth of one of those fanged fish from the black depths at the bottom of the ocean.

"I know we're not taking head readings today but this is too good to pass up."

Flipping through the personal information sheets on the board, Mitch found the original size of the dummy's head and compared it to the new economy size it had become. He raised his eyebrows, noting a 2.2 inch difference in the circumference. He tapped the dummy's head at its temple.

"Probably not a whole lot of thinking going on in there now, eh number 21046? Serves you right for killing your landlady."

The dummy's chest was flattened by the steering wheel. Mitch carefully unzipped the government issued orange jumper. Two ribs on the left side were peeking through the skin and the right side was misshapen and lumpy with the broken bones that hadn't penetrated through the surface tissues. The dummy's abdomen was swollen from internal hemorrhaging, and from the way it was rasping, Mitch could tell its lungs were filling with blood as well. The damage was pretty severe, so it would die relatively quickly, rendering it useless for a second run.

Pulling out a stethoscope, Mitch listened to the last sluggish thumps of the dummy's heart. He looked over at the digital clock on the wall, noting it had been three minutes since the crash. While he was scribbling his remaining findings, Phil sauntered around from the back of the pick-up. He handed Mitch the top sheet from his own clipboard so it would be included in the final report. He glanced at the dummy and grimaced.

"I don't know if I'll ever get used to this, Mitch."

Mitch smirked. "Sure you will. Hey, it took me over a year to get through one of these without puking, so don't feel bad. Besides, you have to think of it this way. They were all gonna get the chair anyway so we might as well get something good from their deaths, am I right?"

Phil shrugged. "I guess I never really thought of that."

"Yeah. It's all about balance, my friend. These guys are all murderers, right? They took something from the world for their own pleasure. So now they gotta give something back. What better way to do that than be part of the research that makes one aspect of the world a safer place for the rest of us? Personally, I think they should all be conscious for it but that's just my opinion."

"Have you ever worked any of these tests when the dummies were awake?"

"Oh, hell yeah. But only a precious few. The dummy's got to be a real rotten son of a bitch to get that sentence. You know, people who kidnap and kill kids. That sorta thing. Speaking of baby killers, lookie what we got here."

Phil looked up as the replacement crew dragged in the new dummy. Kicking and bucking, the new dummy was a thin spindly man with scraggly blonde hair and wild grey eyes. The duct tape over his mouth prevented him from screaming but his jaw was working hard anyway, vulgar curses stifled before they could take form.

Grinning, Mitch grabbed the clipboard and information sheets from one of the replacement crewmen. He instructed them to hold the dummy while the new car, a gas-guzzling oversized SUV, was set into place for a side-impact test. A separate replacement team jogged in to remove the dead convict as a tow-truck hooked up its rig to the demolished pick-up. As both man and machine were dragged off, Mitch approached the writhing prisoner. He clunked the man on the head with the clipboard, grinning.

"Welcome to the Test Area, dummy number 21047. We sure are glad to have you with us today. If you'll please take your seat behind the wheel, we can get the test started. Thank you for participating."

The dummy bucked wildly, screaming behind his duct-tape gag. The replacement team pulled and dragged him towards the SUV. As this one was conscious, they had a tougher time getting him secured behind the wheel. But only after a little struggle, the prisoner was locked in place with portable clamps. Phil clicked the final clamp on the dummy's left wrist and stepped back. Mitch slammed the door, making the prisoner flinch. Subdued now, the man stopped squirming and struggling against his restraints. His eyes widened in terror as Mitch leaned in close and winked.

"How do you feel about setting that busload of kids on fire now, dummy?"

The man whimpered in response. Mitch patted his face and walked over to the control panel. He and Phil pulled on their safety goggles as the red light began to flash. The vehicle was set up for an impact test on the driver's side. The prisoner whipped his head back and forth as if searching for an escape. Finally his gaze locked on the machine positioned 50 feet away that in ten seconds would come hurtling at him at 40mph.

As the test rolled into action, the convict began to cry. His eyes spilled over with hot tears and snot bubbled from his nostrils. As he strained one last time against the clamps he caught Mitch's attention. The supervisor's exaggerated toothy grin and happy thumbs-up gesture helped convince the dummy that there was no escape. He slumped back against the driver's seat and watched as the rapidly approaching cement barrier, its surface crudely painted with the words 'Enjoy The Ride, Dummy' in bright yellow letters, became the slamming door to his new and final prison.

Felicia squeezed the beads of her rosary in her fist. The multiple facets of the red glass left hexagonal imprints on her palm. Felicia found comfort in the Lord, and, as a freshman at St. Katherine's high school, she had plenty of opportunity to seek solace from Him.

From her first day, Felicia became the favorite target of two upper classmen: Tammy Berkshire and Karrie Hendersen. These two seniors found perverse pleasure in making Felicia's daily life a living hell, from morning swirlies to weekly locker sabotage.

Felicia tried to appease them. She'd get them snacks or be the look out when they smoked in the bathroom. She thought it might make things better but despite her efforts, the hazing continued.

So when Tammy offered her a ride home after school, Felicia felt wary. "Hey, Fel. You wanna ride?"

"Why?"

"Why? That's an odd question."

Karrie, who sat on the open passenger side window, giggled.

"I didn't mean anything—"

"Hey," Tammy held up her hands. "If you don't want a ride, I'm not going to force you. I was just trying to be nice."

Felicia bit her bottom lip. If Tammy was being nice and she refused her, the bullying might get worse.

"Okay. I'd love a ride home."

"That's my girl. Hop in!"

Twenty minutes later Tammy drove past Felicia's house and headed for the highway.

"Tammy, that was my house."

"I said I'd take you home, Frosh. I never said when."

Tammy and Karrie ignored her pleas to go home. For hours, Felicia sat clutching her rosary, wishing she'd never gotten in the car. Now, in the dark, Tammy drove them down Dunhill Road, a backwoods dirt lane lined on both sides with tall trees that made Felicia feel as if she were inside a coffin.

"Hey, Fel. You know about this road, right?" Tammy asked.

"No."

Karrie laughed. "You're kidding? You know don't about him?"

"Him?"

"Yeah," Tammy continued. "The Hitchhiker."

"It looks like a hitchhiker but it's not human."

"You mean like a ghost?"

Karrie laughed again.

"Not everyone sees him, you understand. Only those who've been chosen."

"Ch-chosen for what?"

Karrie whispered. "To die."

Felicia gasped and the other girls snickered. Karrie explained.

"It's said that he looks different for everyone. Some say he looks like an old farmer, others like a Union soldier. Could be Satan himself. No matter how he looks, though, if you see him, you don't live to talk about it."

Felicia frowned. "If no one survives, who tells the stories?"

Tammy glared at Felicia in the rearview mirror.

"The point is that certain people see him and those people die. The legend says whomever sees him has a deep dark secret. Something that could ruin lives if it ever got out."

"Yeah," Karrie said. "He sees into you and can tell if you've been a bad girl." "

So, Fel. Is that whole rosary-carrying, God-loving thing real? Or are you hiding behind it?"

The two seniors laughed but Felicia stopped listening. The truth was she did have a secret.

When Felicia was growing up, the woman living down the street from her was a prostitute. No one could prove it, of course. Just watching the men come and go from her place was proof enough. They hid behind the guises of gas company uniforms or dressed as poll takers during elections. Felicia's parents stirred up the neighborhood to alienate the poor woman at every opportunity.

Melody. That was her name. Felicia wondered how someone with such a beautiful name could be a 'filthy whore'. But most of all, she wondered what it was like to be a prostitute. To have sex for money with all different kinds of men? Felicia thought it would be exciting. She thought she would enjoy it.

If her parents ever knew that, they'd kill her. Or themselves. Or both. Suddenly a woman popped into view on the road ahead of them. Felicia could see her white nightgown shine like a star in the black sky. The wind picked up her long chestnut hair and tossed it about. As the car approached, she turned and looked at Felicia, who pressed her hands against the window.

"No," she whispered.

"What?" Tammy said.

"Did you see her?" Felicia asked.

"Her? Her, who?"

"It looked just like Melody."

"I didn't see anyone. Did you, Kar?"

"Nope. I think Fel's losing it."

"Who the hell is—"

Tammy looked in the review mirror and her throat closed, choking off her words. She slammed on the brakes and the Chevy skidded to a halt in a spray of rocks. While Karrie screamed at her, Tammy threw the car into park. She twisted around to get a better look at the back seat.

A lone red beaded rosary lay coiled on the beige leather. Felicia was gone.

MANAH MADE EVIL

"What the heck?"

Adwenia looked down at her husband's shirt and saw the burn mark. She stared at the perforated surface of her electric iron as if she could glean some answer to her current dilemma. Easing the hot iron to the board she turned it off and picked up the now ruined garment. She ground her teeth in frustration.

"I just bought the darned thing. How could it be busted already?"

As she stared at the mark, deciding how rude she would be with the salesperson when she returned the defective iron, Adwenia thought the burn resembled a faded and patchy image. Frowning, she pulled the shirt closer to her nose and inspected it. A faint broken line on the right connected to an arc at the top. She tried to match the pattern to the iron itself but found no similar markings on the appliance.

Sighing, she crumpled the ruined shirt into a ball and threw it into the laundry basket. Tomorrow, after the kids left for school, she would take the iron back to the store. Mark was going to be furious about his favorite shirt.

The next day, she stood in line at the Customer Service desk at Sears. The three elderly women ahead of her were grousing to each other about the shoddy craftsmanship of their recent purchases. Their voices faded into a cacophony of clucking hens, and she tuned them out.

A sudden shove from behind surprised her. Stumbling forward, she fell against one of the older women. As Adwenia straightened, she apologized to the glaring woman then spun around ready to unleash some venom. She faced a young man, bungling with a large plastic bag and wearing a sheepish expression.

"I'm so sorry. I didn't hurt you, did I?"

"No, but you should be more—do I know you?"

"We were standing in line last week. I was buying this rice cooker."

He held up the large plastic bag.

"And you were buying an iron, right?"

Adwenia smiled and held up a paper bag.

"You're joking?" he asked.

"I wish."

As they shared a laugh, one of the complaining women moved up to the service rep and started shouting. The two other ladies nodded as they watched the exchange.

"You'd think the store tried to steal her first born or something. From what I can see, it's a toaster that's gotten her panties in a bunch."

Adwenia chuckled.

"Great. Now I can't that visual out of my head!"

They both cringed as the woman's yelling turned to shrieks and another store employee joined the discussion.

She turned away from the spectacle to talk to the young man.

"The mall was packed with shoppers last week. How did you remember me?"

"I'm normally really good with faces but it was something else that made you stand out. Remember that lady whose little kid was kicking up such a fuss?"

"Of course. Everyone in the store was giving her the evil eye. I just felt so sorry for her."

"That's exactly my point. You were the only one that was nice to her. You said something about when your kids were that age."

"And you remember that?"

"That kind of stuff always catches my attention. A person being understanding, compassionate, just human. You're probably a really good mom, too."

Adwenia laughed.

"Well, I don't know about that. You'd have to ask my kids."

"No, you can't fool me. I bet you're always sacrificing for them, too."

"That's what it means to be a parent."

He held up a hand. "I didn't mean that in a bad way, honest."

She smiled and he looked relieved.

"Let me buy you a coffee when we're done here."

"I don't know. I've got so much to do at home."

"Oh, come on. It's just coffee. We can swap appliance debacle stories."

She felt herself smiling again, her cheeks flushing with heat, then nodded.

"All right. Sounds fun."

That afternoon, Adwenia tried a new iron. She found

herself thinking about Manny, the young man she'd met at the store. His hazel eyes, framed by long dark lashes, complimented his olive skin. She wanted to run her fingers through his jet wavy hair and allow his slender graceful fingers trace her—

She shook her head. What was she doing? Fantasizing about a man half her age while ironing her *husband's* shirts? She pulled the iron back and saw another burn mark on the crisp lavender cotton. Grumbling she shut the iron off and slammed it onto the board.

"Are you kidding me?"

Holding up the shirt, she studied this burn. It was similar to the last one but more defined: a solid line with two grips on the right attached to a gently sloping arced blade. It looked like a scythe. She dropped the shirt in a panic. The fabric landed burn side up, its one small section smooth and even. Turning away from the shirt, she stared at the iron.

"What is going on?"

She pulled one of her son's thin t-shirts from the laundry basket and put it on the board. Crazy or not, she didn't want to ruin three of Mark's good shirts. She flipped the iron back on, then stretched the shirt over the rim of the board. Even if this one burned, Eric wouldn't care. He had a drawer full of them that he'd barely worn. When the iron was hot enough, she laid it on the garment.

She pulled it away and the scythe began forming again. Chewing on her lip, she pressed the iron down for another five seconds. This time, the iron left more details. What looked like wood grain appeared on the staff, and a slight gleam shone on the blade. Her heart began to pound as she pressed the iron down again, this time for half a minute.

Within the burn she could now see the grips were worn

from much use, ridged in a pattern that would fit a skeletal hand. The tang, where the blade joined the staff, was wrapped in brown stained leather and adorned with small bones and feathers. The blade's sharp edge reflected an unseen light from above. She could squinted while looking at it.

"*Mom.* What are you doing?"

She dropped the t-shirt. Her son stood there, his face screwed up into a scowl. She hadn't heard the kids come home. He picked up the shirt and shook it at her, his voice infuriated.

"Are you *trying* to ruin my shirt?"

Heat surged through her chest. She slapped Eric hard enough to make him drop the shirt and cradle his cheek. Adwenia stepped forward and pushed her nose against his. He was three inches taller and 20 pounds heavier but she was his mother which still carried weight in his teenage mind.

"Don't you *ever* raise your voice to me again. Even if I wanted to ruin your clothes on purpose, which I *didn't*, I can. You know why? Because I paid for them. You've got a hundred other shirts so I'm sure you'll survive without this one. Now get your ass to your room *RIGHT NOW*."

She had backed Eric into the corner. He scuttled past her, ran up to the second floor and slammed the door. She blinked and shook herself. Regret washed over her and she stared at the staircase. What was wrong with her? Eric didn't deserve such vicious treatment.

She stepped away from the ironing board but before she could go upstairs her daughter, Emily, spoke.

"Don't, Mom. Just let him cool off a bit, okay?"

She turned to see her daughter standing in the entryway to the kitchen, an open carton of yogurt in her hand. She looked distraught. Adwenia approached her and smoothed a hand over Emily's hair.

"I...I don't know what happened. I've never done that, to anyone, before."

"You can't be perfect all the time, you know. Besides, he was being a douche."

Emily began to smile but Adwenia knocked the yogurt from her hand.

"Don't be such a vulgar whore, Em."

Emily stared at her mother. Adwenia grabbed Emily's arm and bent her down toward the spilled food. Her voice was cold.

"Clean it up."

As she moved back to the ironing board, she could hear Emily sniffling behind her. Ignoring her daughter, Adwenia grabbed the iron and laid a pair of cotton shorts on the board.

By the time Mark returned home from work, Adwenia had burned through enough clothing to fill the laundry basket. With each garment the details on the scythe became more intricate and letters had begun to appear. Too faint at this point but she continued grabbing any and all pieces of clothing she could.

She was just beginning to see the letters 'd-i' on Emily's pink sweatpants when someone grabbed her arm and spun her around. Mark shook her several times before she realized who he was. He was shouting at her.

"*Winny.* Winny, what are you doing?"

"I—" she replied as she turned back to the ironing board. Mark shook her again.

"Winny. Look at me."

She finally focused on her husband, blinked, then smiled.

"Mark, what are you doing home so early?"

"It's six o'clock."

"No, that can't be right. I just started ironing a few minutes ago."

Mark spun her around to face the picture window in the living room.

"Look. It's dark outside."

Her forehead crinkled in a frown. *How was this possible?* She heard Eric and Emily close their bedroom doors and come down to the living room. She stared at them as they eyed her warily. Emily was glaring at her. Eric wouldn't meet her eyes. Mark turned to look at them.

"Kids, how long has your mother been in here?"

"She was ironing when we got home from school," Emily said. "Then she freaked out, hit Eric, and called me a whore."

Mark released Adwenia's arm and turned to look at her.

"What the hell is going on, Winny?"

She shook her head. Her memories were fuzzy at best. Just then a soft whisper sounded in her ear.

"Adwenia."

Adwenia twitched, then looked around the room.

"Did you hear that?"

"Hear what, Winny?"

Adwenia looked down at the iron and she heard the voice again.

"Adwenia."

She grabbed the iron and pressed it down on the sweatpants. Mark tried to pull her away but she screamed at him and shook him off.

"Don't you hear it? It's trying to talk to me!"

When she lifted the iron, a complete word had been burned into the fabric alongside the scythe.

DIE.

She stepped back from the board, shaking her head.

"What's does it mean? Am I going to die? Is someone else?"

"Winny, what are you talking about?"

She spun around to look at Mark, pointing at the board.

"Are you trying to tell me you can't see that?"

"See what?"

She grabbed his shirt collar and pulled him forward.

"That burn mark and the word next to it!"

"Winny, all I see are the sweatpants. They aren't burned."

She pounded her finger directly on top of the scythe blade and looked at Mark. He eyed the pants again but shook his head.

"There's nothing there, Win."

"How can you not—"

Looking down, Adwenia felt her face slacken in disbelief. She saw nothing. No scythe, no word, no burns. She clutched her hands to her chest.

"But it was there. I saw...it burned your shirt yesterday so I exchanged the iron but the image came back. I swear it was there, Mark."

She began to cry. "I don't understand."

Mark wrapped her in his arms and held her close.

"It's all right, Winny. It'll be all right. We can have Dr. Stephens check you out tomorrow, okay?"

She nodded against his chest and relaxed. The afternoon's events flooded back. From threatening her son to her cruelty against her daughter to the hours she spent standing over the ironing board believing she had ruined her family's clothes. She pushed away from Mark and looked at her children. Her eyes spilled over with tears.

"Oh my God, Eric. Emily. I am so sorry. I didn't mean anything I said earlier. I promise. I don't know what came over me."

Eric's eyes welled with tears and he ran into her arms. She embraced him as if someone was trying to steal him away and in seconds he gasped in her ear.

"Mom...can't breathe..."

She released him. "Oh, I'm sorry, Eric. Are you all right?"

He nodded and smiled at her. She looked at Emily.

"Can you forgive me?"

Emily squinted her eyes at her mother but with a curt nod from Mark, Emily walked slowly to her mother and hugged her. She didn't cling like Eric, but Adwenia squeezed her tight. When she looked down at her daughter, Emily was smiling.

"I promise I'll never speak to you that way again. Either of you."

Mark, Eric, and Emily seemed satisfied and happy again. Adwenia wiped the tears from her face and clapped her hands.

"Okay. Who wants pizza?"

They all mumbled 'hooray' at the same time. As they moved into the kitchen, Adwenia grabbed her purse and pulled out her wallet. She dug through the many compartments until she found her doctor's business card. She stuck it under a magnet on the refrigerator.

After the kids were asleep and Mark lay in bed reading, she went through the house turning off lights and checking the doors. After setting the security alarm she heard her cell phone ring. Digging it out of her purse, she checked the number. Her heart fluttered for a brief moment before she answered.

"Manny?"

"Hi, Adwenia. What's up?"

"Uh, I'm getting ready to sleep. It's after eleven."

"Oh, wow. I didn't realize it was so late. I'll make this quick then. I was wondering if you wanted to have lunch tomorrow."

"I don't know. I've got to call my doctor and see if I can get an appointment tomorrow but otherwise, I think my schedule is free."

"Doctor? Are you all right?"

"It's nothing for you to worry about. Can I get back to you tomorrow?"

"Sure thing. I'll talk to you then, Winny. Sleep tight."

"Good night, Manny."

After she hung up, she realized he called her Winny. Only Mark ever called her that. Her heart quickened again and she fanned herself with her hand as she walked back upstairs.

The following day, her doctor scheduled her for three o-clock. She called Manny and set up a lunch date for noon.

As he nibbled on a chicken salad sandwich, Adwenia sipped her second margarita, something she rarely did. The alcohol warmed her stomach, making her tipsy despite being full of complimentary bread.

Manny put down his fork, folded his hands under his chin and looked at her.

"I know it's probably none of my business but what's with this doctor appointment? You're not sick are you? I mean like seriously ill?"

Maybe it was the tequila, but she told him the truth.

"No, it's not that. I'm more sick up here."

She tapped at her temple. Manny frowned.

"You're sick in the head?"

Adwenia laughed and nodded.

"That's the best way to put it. I keep seeing things, hearing things. I've been acting out against my family."

Adwenia shivered and gripped the glass in front of her.

"I'm not like that. I'm probably the most even keeled person I know but the things I've said and done...There's something wrong."

"What kind of things have you seen?"

"It doesn't matter. It's crazy, I know that now."

Manny reached over and touched her hand, a soft delicate stroke of his fingers against hers. What felt like a small electric shock buzzed up her arm and she blinked. The restaurant blurred around her until all she could see were the details of Manny's eyes. Flecks of green swam in his warm brown irises, giving the illusion of movement. Or were they really swirling, flashing green light that melted into red and orange, like a raging fire...

"Winny?"

She shook her head and everything came back into focus. Manny was holding her hand, his brow a creased canvas of worry.

"Winny, are you all right?"

"Yeah, yeah. I'm fine. What was I talking about?"

He leaned forward, whispering, "You were telling me about the messages you're getting from the iron."

"I was?"

Manny nodded. "I don't think you're crazy, Winny, because I've been getting some, too."

Adwenia smiled. She almost felt vindicated.

"Where? What have they said?"

"Well, not from my iron. In the bathtub. When I use that scrubbing bubble stuff, images keep popping up. Then, yesterday, I started seeing letters."

"That's exactly what's been happening to me, too."

"It's why I called you. I wanted to talk to you about this. I don't know why but I feel very comfortable around you, Winny. I didn't trust my other friends or family to believe me."

She gripped his hand in hers and he smiled.

"I know what you mean, Manny."

"Anyway, yesterday the bubbles spelled out D-I-E. I don't know if that means I'm going to die or someone else is or what."

"Oh my God that's what I saw, too."

"See, Winny? You're not crazy. You don't need a doctor. You just need to keep focusing on the iron."

"You're right. I just need to keep focusing."

She pulled out her cell phone and dialed her doctor's office. After cancelling her afternoon appointment, Adwenia abruptly ended the call then turned off her phone. She smiled at Manny and stood.

"I don't meant to be rude but I think I should get back home. The iron is waiting."

"Of course, Winny. It's for the best. Don't worry about the check. I'll take care of it. I'll take care of everything."

Once Adwenia arrived home, she immediately plugged in the iron and gathered a basket full of clothes while it warmed up. She put one of Mark's work shirts on the board and set the iron on top. After five minutes, she lifted it and the word 'die' was scorched, thick and black, into the fabric. Below it, though, the first faint marks of another letter were forming. She put the iron back down and waiting ten minutes more.

By the time she had worked her way through four baskets of clothes, the message was complete: D-I-E F-A-M-I-L-Y S-A-V-E S-E-L-F. Though a fraction of her brain was telling her she needed a doctor, the rest of her understood the dire message. Of course, it made sense now. They were all against her. They've probably been plotting against her for years. Mark with his mumbled comments about her weight or eating habits. The kids always whining and bitching about her lack of cooking skills or comparing her to their friends' moms.

They all wanted her put away in a nut house. Wasn't it Mark's suggestion for her to see a doctor? They hoped she would be committed, to get her out of the way for someone better or prettier or younger. The last part of the message, though, was 'save self'. Would an institution be far enough out of the way for them? Would they be willing to kill her, make sure she was gone forever? Adwenia had no doubt as to their intentions but she wasn't going quietly.

Eric arrived home from school first. Emily wouldn't be far behind so she had to act fast. As he came through the front door, calling out to her, she ran at him from the kitchen. She hefted a rolling pin over her head and slammed iy against his temple just as he turned to look. He didn't have a chance to be surprised before slumping to the ground. She tried to slam the door closed but it rammed Eric's ankle with loud crack. She dragged him back into the foyer, quickly closed the door, then pulled him into the living room.

When Emily came home fifteen minutes later, Adwenia was waiting behind the door. She didn't need to hide as her daughter's face was buried in her phone while she texted or twittered. Moving to the living room, Emily tripped and fell forward. Her phone flew to the side as she threw out her arms to brace her fall.

Landing on her stomach, she grunted as her body slammed to the floor, the carpet burning her chin as she slid against it. She quickly rolled over on her side and looked back, determined to kick or yell at whatever made her fall. When she saw her brother, throat slit wide open, skin pale and ashen against the spreading pool of blood surrounding his corpse, Emily screamed. She scrabbled over to her brother and gently shook him.

"Eric? No, no, no. Eric, come on. *Eric.*"

As Adwenia stepped forward, Emily turned to see her mother standing in the foyer.

"Mom. Help me. *Eric's dead.*"

Adwenia moved further into the living room and Emily finally saw the bloodied butcher knife clenched in her mother's hand. The confusion on her daughter's face made her grin. She held up the knife and took another step toward Emily.

"Mom?"

Emily lunged backward toward the kitchen but Adwenia caught her by the hair and slammed her to the floor. Emily screamed once for help before Adwenia plunged the knife into her daughter's throat. It passed through the soft flesh and stuck in the floor beneath. She left it there and walked to the kitchen to get the cleaver.

Thirty minutes later, Emily lay in pieces next to her brother. Adwenia stood over the corpses of her children and smiled. A slight hiss and pop sounded from the corner and she saw a thin trail of smoke wafting up from the iron. Frowning, Adwenia dropped the cleaver and walked over to the iron. She lifted it to reveal a triangular shaped burn on the ironing board cover.

"What?"

Adwenia grabbed a shirt and stretched it flat. She pressed the iron on it, making sure to crank the heat to the highest setting, and waited for five minutes. When she lifted the iron, no burn mark appeared. Confused, she put it down again and waited another five minutes. She continued this rhythm for over an hour but still nothing appeared on the shirt—no regular burn marks, no messages, nothing.

"I don't understand."

She never heard the approaching sirens as she stood in her living room, screaming at the iron, demanding it tell her what to do next. As the front door crashed open, as several police officers surrounded her, even as they cuffed her, Adwenia continued shrieking at the iron. It wasn't until she was forced through the front door that she realized she was being arrested.

A small group of neighbors and lookie-loos gathered outside her home to gawk and whisper to each other about the spectacle. Adwenia spotted Manny near the end of the driveway and shouted to him.

"Manny! Manny, you've got to help me. Tell them what's going on. About the iron and the messages! I had to do it, didn't I? The iron told me! Manny!"

Manny looked around and behind him, his face a contorted map of confusion. He pointed at his chest and mouthed *Me?* as Adwenia stared at him. She watched as he shook his head and shared a private comment with the person standing next to him. As she was pushed down into the backseat of the cruiser, the last thing Adwenia saw was the wicked smiled on Manny's face.

Akem Manah watched the police haul Adwenia away. Even as the car drove down the street, he could see her twist and turn in the back seat, trying to look at him and plead for help. When she left 'Manny' at the restaurant, he had quickly paid the bill and followed her home. He sat in his car and watched her through the window as she laid iron to cloth all afternoon. When she ambushed her son, Akem knew he'd been successful in twisting another mortal's mind to his will.

It wasn't until after Adwenia slaughtered Emily that he used a cell phone to call the police and report the attacks. He smiled to himself when the police arrived. He had to refrain from giggling as Adwenia was escorted from the house and called out to him. And now, just as the emergency personnel were rolling sheet covered bodies into a waiting ambulance, Mark's car screeched to a halt at the base of his driveway.

Akem was tempted to intervene in some way, to add another notch to his warped mind bedpost. But as Mark collapsed to his knees, sobbing as his children's corpses rolled past, Akem knew there'd be no challenge in that. He sniffed the air and could almost taste Mark's broken spirit.

The remaining crowd paid him no mind as Akem Manah slowly walked away and disappeared into the fading afternoon light.

Grams stood naked in the yard for three days. Whitney watched her as she shuffled outside on Friday morning and stared off into the distance. The sun beat down on her thin shoulders during the day. The sliver of moon at night barely gave her a glance. Now the black rain has come again and Grams will die.

Thunder echoed through the empty neighborhood as dark clouds roiled with violent energy. Her skin blistered and cracked from exposure, Grams stood in the rain, her snow white hair plastered in black ribbons against her skull. Rivulets of ebony, like tiny oil slicks, trickled down her breasts, along her thighs, and into the ground.

When all this started, people had flocked to their congressmen, police, churches and clergy with their questions fueled by awe, fear, and panic. Google failed within twelve hours as people flooded cyber space searching for answers. Facebook and Twitter took a whole day. Within a week the Internet ceased to exist.

It didn't matter anyway. One quarter of the world's population lay dead or disintegrating two weeks after that.

Six months later, you *could* swing a dead cat without hitting another living soul. Whitney figured she and Grams remained the last people left alive in the world.

The damned rain. It only takes a single drop against bare skin for the destruction of the soul to begin. Passing through the human body the rain takes every bit that is you until only the mass of cells remains, like spent grounds left in a coffee filter. And when that last spark is gone the remaining flesh falls away. Like you never existed at all.

Father Franklin explained everything in that last sermon, the one only Whitney and Grams attended, about the war in Heaven. His watery eyes spilled tears when he described that the angels fought each other over us. His shoulders trembled when he said they a started civil war to prove how minuscule or mighty we should be in the eyes of God. And as he shook his Bible above his head, Father screamed that our demise lay at the feet of their timeless capacity to hold a grudge.

That afternoon, as Grams and Whitney arrived home, a thick, heavy front of clouds suddenly appeared above them. Between the flashes of lightening, Whitney spotted dozens of dark winged shapes twisting and rolling in battle. She watched one plummet to the earth in defeat, a long fiery trail marking its trajectory.

The charred remains of the heavenly creature mixed with the sheets of rain as the storm progressed. Whitney tried to pull her grandmother into the house despite the older woman's continued slow and steady pace. But when the first black drops spattered Grams' arms, Whitney released her and ducked through the door to the enclosed porch. Pressing her face against the glass she watched as Grams slowly moved up the steps then stopped with her hand on the door knob. When she looked up at Whitney, the slack expression on her face said it all.

That was the beginning of the end for Grams.

Now Monday afternoon, hours after the storm started, the clouds above began to clear, a small circle spinning ever wider revealing a swath of grey sky. The rains moved with the clouds and soon stopped all together. Whitney stared through the front door at the yard. To the right of the small steps leading from the house, next to a dead evergreen bush, sat the metal bucket and scoop.

Smudgy remnants of black goo stained the bottom. Residue of her parents.

Her folks had been caught unprepared when the rains first came, walking home from their weekly Bridge game two streets over. Soaked from head to toe by the time they'd shambled into the front yard, they'd simply laid down. Two days later the rain came again and took them away.

Whitney, her brother Pat, and Grams fended for themselves for several months before he'd had enough. He walked outside while the winds from an approaching black storm raged around him. Pat screamed his fury at the sky then put their dad's .9mm in his mouth and blew out the back of his skull. He remained in the yard for three days before Whitney realized the rain hadn't taken his soul so it would have no effect on his body. It took her all day to dig a grave with her skinny chicken arms, something Pat had teased her about endlessly. By dinner time, she had him wrapped and laid to rest.

She stared at Grams. The older woman swayed on her feet but she could see the tears beginning to form in her wrinkled skin. As rips pulled open on Grams' head, Whitney automatically stepped back. The bodily fluids couldn't hurt her but Grams still had black rain trickling over her skin. Despite the protection provided by the glass and wood door, fear dictated Whitney's movements. It only took a drop...

Grams' skin suit began to pile up around her ankles as it slipped off her muscles. Tendons and ligaments twanged and snapped as they released their attachments to bone. Her flesh bubbled and melted, crawling down her body in a gelatinous mass and resting at her feet. The remaining skeleton, thin and covered in small fractures, popped and shifted. It disappeared in a burst of dust, the powder mixing with the rain and turning to sludge as it settled into the wet ground.

Sighing, Whitney turned to the box of disposable hazmat suits next to the door. She'd found them a few months back on one of her scavenging runs. While the local hospital had been picked clean of most of its antibiotics and pain killers, an entire storeroom of protective gear sat untouched. After seeing what happened to her folks, Whitney knew these could save her life just as much as bottled water and canned food.

She stepped into one of the suits, yanked the hood over her head, and pulled the zipper up to her chin. Throwing on a pair of elbow length plastic gloves, Whitney used duct tape to secure them. She did the same at the ankles of the suit after tucking them into a thick pair of socks. She slipped into knee high boots.

Securing a plastic shield to her head, she moved outside. She felt clunky and awkward, like a dog forced to wear booties to protect its sensitive paws from the cold, but she couldn't be too careful.

Whitney stepped over to her grams' remains and stared down at them.

The human soup gurgling at her feet no longer made

her feel nauseated. Within minutes she'd scooped the slop into the bucket and hauled it to the backyard. She'd already dug a hole next to the rest of the family plots. She poured Grams in. Hard to believe it had only been fifteen minutes since she liquefied. Whitney made a half attempt at crossing herself—an automatic response drilled into her since grade school—before she returned the bucket to the stoop. The disposable suit and gloves went into the trash.

Her evening meal of stale bread, small hunk of cheese, and flat pop tasted like ash on her tongue as tears dampened her cheeks.

The following weeks passed by in a blur of inactivity. Without family, friends, or even strangers coming by, Whitney found herself roaming the streets, circling farther out each day. She'd have to find a bike or a car soon if she wanted to explore beyond her own neighborhood. For now, as long as she carried her safety gear with her, she could wander until exhaustion forced her back home.

One afternoon, as she sat under a giant oak tree in the city park nibbling on a peanut butter sandwich, distant thunder rolled across the sky. Whitney stared to the west and saw a front of black clouds swirling toward her. She quickly opened her backpack and pulled on the protective wear. Once taped and secured, she could safely gather her belongings. As she tied the pack closed and slung it over her shoulder, another sound hit her ears. Not thunder but more like—

She spun around to see a long line of Airstreams, like a shiny centipede, crawling its way through the center of town. Squeaking out a small gasp of surprise Whitney bolted toward them, the pack bouncing up and down on her back. The RVs were still a long way off but she had several long blocks to cover before she reached the main road.

The skies opened up and a heavy deluge of blackness rained down. Whitney continually wiped her gloved hand across the plastic visor in order to see the pavement below her. With just a block to go, a low hanging branch snagged her pack and pulled it from her shoulders. She left it behind and pumped her arms and legs, moving as fast as she could toward the approaching caravan.

Something small and cool tickled along her arm and her running slowed.

She gamely jogged as she stared down at the tear in her suit and the black rain sprinkling against her skin. Easing to a walk, she stuck a finger inside the suit's hole, wondering at the dark water. The protective face shield tumbled off her head and clattered to the sidewalk. Tiny black rivers cascaded across her face and down into the suit.

"Huh."

When she reached the corner, she stopped and let her arms hang at her sides. Moments later the convoy of RVs roared into view. She stared at the cluster of surprised faces gathered at one of the vehicle's windows as it rolled past. The final camper slowed to a stop and she turned to look at the pitiful gaze of the driver. The young man stared at her then shook his head and drove away, catching up to the rest of the group.

Whitney stood in the rain and watched the line of RVs disappear over the horizon.

The wail pierced the heavy blanket of sleep that enfolded Deirdre. She was startled into consciousness so suddenly that she almost forgot where she was. But when the next desperate cry sounded from the other end of the house, she remembered all too well. Slipping out from beneath the covers, Deirdre reached over and lit the bedside candle. Pulling a wool shawl around her thin shoulders and pushing her feet into her slippers, she carried the candle and a dark glass bottle to the door.

Walking out into the hall, another mournful cry echoed down the dark passage. Weakly, Deirdre called out. "I'm coming, Mother."

She approached the open doorway on her left. Deirdre could hear the pitiful sobbing that wracked her mother's disease-weakened body. Since the spring, Margaret (Maggie to her friends) McIntyre had been slowly but surely wasting away, her body being consumed at a steady pace by cancer. And in 1818, with very little in the way of trained, or even sanitary, medical practices, Maggie's only relief was through drug-induced oblivion, which Deirdre carried in the glass bottle.

Now, in the heart of winter, Maggie was nothing more than a skeleton in a bag of skin that was sallow and milk-white at the same time. If she studied her mother closely, Deirdre could almost make out the exact contours of Maggie's skull and the hollows of her eye sockets. Her hipbones jutted up from the concave surface of her lower abdomen. Her fingers had withered into knobby claws, not unlike the black and leafless tree branches tapping at the bedroom window. Her feet, next to the stick-like visage of her legs and ankles, looked swollen and distorted, her only features to appear bigger since the disease took over.

Standing in the doorway, studying her mother's emaciated face, Deirdre sighed. Through her pain-ridden delirium, Maggie slowly turned her head to look at her daughter. Reaching out weakly, Maggie whispered urgently to Deirdre. "Oh, Pamela. Come quickly. The horses are running through my room again. You know how that will upset Papa."

Deirdre shook her head sadly. She was used to her mother's addled brain. If the pain wasn't causing her hallucinations and confusion, it was the opium-laced compound the doctor prescribed to keep her "comfortable."

"No, Mother, it's me. Deirdre."

Angrily, her mother argued. "I don't know any Deirdre. Who are you? Why are you in my house?"

"I'm your daughter. You've been sick and I'm taking care of you, remember?" she asked, exasperated at having to explain again.

Maggie frowned but recognition dawned on her sunken face. "Oh, Deirdre. There you are. Where have you been? I've been calling you for hours."

Deirdre sighed and shook her head. Her mother's sense of time was completely distorted by the pain. What was actually only minutes, seemed like hours to Maggie. An hour felt like a day. That's what pain did to a person. That was its sole purpose. It sucked up thought and reason so it was impossible to decipher anything except when it hurt and when it didn't. There was no more day or night, light or dark, asleep or awake. There was only pain or no pain. It gobbled up birthdays, anniversaries, the turning of the seasons, and even time itself just as the disease was feasting upon her mother's flesh.

Sitting on the edge of the bed, Deirdre reached for her mother and propped her up on the pillows. Making a feeble attempt at the bottle still in Deirdre's grip, Maggie's trembling hand was not quick enough to snatch the medicine from her daughter. In fact, Deirdre smacked the back of Maggie's hand like you would a child who was trying to sneak a cookie before supper. Maggie moaned. Deirdre's voice was stagnant with contempt and irritation.

"Mother, be patient. I have to measure this out precisely. Do you remember what the doctor said? No, of course you don't. We must be very careful not to give you too much. It might kill you and we wouldn't want that, would we?"

Deirdre gave her mother a sharp pointed look, conveying the warning with her eyes, as well as her words. Maggie shook her head back and forth, fearful that Deirdre might delay further in relieving the pain. She watched her daughter while she measured out a spoonful of the dark liquid as a greedy vulture would watch a man on the verge of death, struggling through the desert, knowing it was only a matter of time before it could feast on his flesh. As Deirdre put the bottle on the bedside table, Maggie unconsciously reached out for the spoon. When Deirdre turned back, she bumped into her mother's hand and spilled most of the medicine on the white bedcovers.

Unable to contain it any longer, Deirdre's rage boiled to the surface. Her mother cringed into her pillows, as if it were possible to melt into and beyond them, out of the room, to escape her daughter's wrath. Deirdre screamed.

"Mother! Look what you've done! How many times do we have to go through this? Every day it's the same thing. You cannot administer the medicine yourself. You are too sick and weak. Do you not think me capable? Have I not been taking care of you for almost a year now?"

With each word she leaned closer to Maggie. Her last words brought her inches from her mother's face. Deirdre's own face was purple with hatred. The last 10 months of caring for her mother had taken its toll. She hated her mother for being sick. She hated having to cook her meals and then clean up her vomit when her stomach couldn't digest the food. She hated cleaning out the chamber pot after her mother was able to get out of bed and the soiled bed sheets when she couldn't. Deirdre no longer had a life of her own and she hated Maggie for it.

But the worst of it all was Michael. Michael was the love of her life and the most beautiful man she'd ever known. He was the first and only man to fall in love with her and propose marriage. She emphasized the 'was' in her mind because Michael was gone. He'd wanted to get married last March and move out west to take over his uncle's cattle ranch. But when Maggie took ill, Deirdre was the only family she had to care for her, so she couldn't go.

She begged him to wait out the year. Maggie surely wouldn't last through the winter and then they could go away and be happy together—forever. But Michael had to take over the ranch right away. His Uncle had died in January and had no family. Michael was the rightful heir but if he didn't claim the ranch by April, the local bank would buy out the mortgage to it and sell it to the highest bidder. It was his best chance at a future and he had to take it.

The last Deirdre had heard from him was in July and he and his new wife were doing well. Sorry things turned out this way, he still loved her but he hoped she understood, and so on and so on. Thinking back on the day she received that letter, Deirdre remembered hearing her heart shatter like a crystal goblet dropped on a marble floor. Her soul grew dark that day and she turned her love for Michael into hatred for her mother.

Deirdre grabbed her mother's wrists in her hands. She squeezed until Maggie whimpered from the new pain. She squeezed harder until Maggie was silent. Her tear-filled eyes searched her daughter's for a hint of mercy and compassion but found none. Deirdre's eyes were dark and almost unreadable with anger. They were alien to Maggie. Understanding finally dawned on her and she realized pain was not her greatest fear now. It was Deirdre.

Deirdre released her grip on Maggie and walked to the end of the room, leaving the spilled medicine to soak into the bed sheets and the thinly coated spoon just out of her mother's reach. Maggie didn't even attempt to reach for either the spoon or the bottle on the table. She only watched with trepidation as Deirdre paced back and forth along the foot of the bed. Every now and again Deirdre would look over at her mother, her eyes squinted in disgust, as if she had just discovered a dead rodent in the pantry.

Suddenly she stopped pacing. She turned quickly and walked up to the foot of the bed. She put her hands on the footboard and studied her mother for several long minutes. Just as Maggie was about to ask her what she was doing, Deirdre's mouth curled up into a sly cruel smile. It lasted only a moment and then her features softened with sympathy and, seemingly, guilt. But Maggie had seen it. She saw the cruelty hidden behind the mask of the dutiful daughter. Gazing up at Deirdre as she approached the bedside, Maggie knew she would be dead by morning.

"Oh, Mother. I am sorry. I...I don't know what's come over me. Can you ever forgive me? Here, let me get you some medicine."

Deirdre opened the bottle and measured out another spoonful for Maggie.

Clutching her hands to her chest, Maggie never took her eyes off her daughter's face. She swallowed the syrup with an audible gulp and Deirdre smiled sweetly. Maggie mirrored the smile but not the cunning behind it. If Deirdre was to be her deliverer from the pain, so be it. There was nothing she could, or wanted, to do about it now. Resigning herself to the inevitable, she reached out a trembling hand to her daughter and brushed a finger along her cheek. Caught off guard by the sudden display of affection, Deirdre's anger was diffused as a frown creased her brow.

"My darling. I know this hasn't been easy for you. You've given up your own life to care for me and I will never forget it. You are my only child, Deirdre. I love you very much. Do what you feel you must. But know this: if you go through with it, you will never be at peace, in this life or the next."

Deirdre coughed nervously and stammered out a reply, blinking rapidly and looking everywhere but at Maggie. "What are you talking about, Mother?"

Maggie did not answer. She only cupped her daughter's

cheek in her hand and smiled. Tired from the pain and with the medicine making her drowsy, she dropped her hand to her lap and closed her eyes. As sleep pulled at the corners of her consciousness, she mumbled her final words to Deirdre.

"No peace, my darling daughter. Now or ever. No... peace."

As Maggie relaxed into painless sleep, Deirdre tensed with anger, and not a little fear. She clenched her hands into fists and pounded them against her thighs. It was impossible. How could she have known her intentions? The idea to kill her mother had only occurred to her minutes ago. It's not as if she had been planning this for months. Of course, being raised in a strict, Catholic home, murdering her mother would leave quite a stain on her soul. But it really would be a mercy killing, Deirdre reasoned with herself. Maggie had suffered so long with the pain and Deirdre could release her. Surely God would understand. If He didn't, well, then at least Maggie wouldn't be the only one freed from this misery.

She stopped hammering her fists. Leaning over, she spoke softly in Maggie's ear.

"Mother? Are you awake?"

Upon hearing her daughter's voice, Maggie frowned and whimpered softly in her sleep. But in just a few moments, her face smoothed and relaxed and she even smiled a little. Deirdre's lip curled up in a vicious snarl again as she slowly pulled one of the down pillows from behind her mother's head. Fueled by her frustrations, and the incredulity that her mother knew what she had planned, she pressed the pillow over Maggie's face.

At first nothing was happening. Deirdre expected her mother to thrash or struggle in some way. Just as she was about to reposition the pillow, Maggie twitched. After applying a bit more pressure, Deirdre watched as the feeble twitching turned more violent. Maggie's hands clawed at the pillow as she struggled to push it away. Her legs, even in such a weakened and atrophied state, thrashed with a strength Deirdre thought impossible. She threw her whole upper body over the pillow as she was afraid her mother might actually succeed in slipping out from beneath it.

Eventually, Maggie stopped kicking. Her arms fell at her sides and her body was utterly motionless. Deirdre kept the pillow over Maggie's face long after she lay still. Shaking from the effort, Deirdre slowly pulled away the pillow. Her mother's eyes were half closed and her jaw sagged open. Without really thinking, Deirdre reached over and smoothed her hand over Maggie's face, pulling down on her eyelids.

Closing her own eyes, Deirdre breathed a heavy sigh of relief. Looking back down at her mother, a small gasp escaped her lips. Maggie's eyes were open. Deirdre pulled the eyelids down again only to watch in horror as they slowly opened again. After trying to close them a third time, a small smile tugged at Deirdre's mouth. She quickly walked to the front hall and grabbed her change purse. Shaking her head and laughing softly, she pulled out two silver coins. Rubbing them together as she walked back to her mother's room, she scolded herself for being so skittish.

Placing the coins over her mother's eyes, Deirdre smiled. "There we go, Mother. Isn't that better?" Shaking a finger at her mother's corpse, Deirdre scolded the dead woman. "You shouldn't scare your daughter like that. For a moment, I almost believed you were still alive. Then I'd be forced to kill you all over again and the good Lord knows how exhausted I am from the first effort."

Adjusting the wool shawl around her shoulders and

sighing in contentment, she picked up the candle on the bedside table. Walking to the window opposite the bed, Deirdre hummed quietly. She put the candle on the small wooden table beneath the window and gazed out into the night. Deciding to get a breath of fresh air, she leaned over to push open the window. A small corner of the shawl dipped into the flame of the lit candle. It was half-eaten by fire by the time Deirdre realized it. The upper portion of her nightdress was also quickly engulfed.

When Deirdre released her first agonizing scream, her hair was set afire, along with her kerchief. It seared directly to her scalp, which quickly blackened. Soon all the layers of her clothing were on fire and clung mercilessly to her body. Her skin sizzled and cracked, her flesh bubbled. The small table she leaned upon for support caught fire and added to the blaze. Deirdre whirled and spun, hoping to put out the fire, but it was too late. Her screams echoed throughout the house until her vocal chords melted and slid down her throat like a boiling glob of oyster flesh.

In her final pain-racked moments, she turned towards her mother's corpse.

Her bloodied and blistered mouth opened in a silent cry of rage and she flung herself on the deathbed, tearing and beating at Maggie's body. The last thing she saw, before her eyes exploded from the heat, was the angelic perfection of her mother's face, haloed in fire and burnt bedclothes, smiling in the sweet repose of peace and retribution.

In time, Deirdre slumped and lay quietly on her mother's breast. Her suffering subsided into a more annoying vibration at the back of her skull than actual pain. She felt as if she were floating in a lake of warm water, weightless and adrift. She was angry at having to die, but, she thought to herself, at least I'm free. I'm free. Then everything went white.

The wail pierced the heavy blanket of sleep that enfolded Deirdre. She was startled into consciousness so suddenly that she almost forgot where she was. But when the next desperate cry sounded from the other end of the house, she remembered all too well. Slipping out from beneath the covers, Deirdre reached over and lit the bedside candle. Pulling a wool shawl around her thin shoulders and pushing her feet into her slippers, she carried the candle and a dark glass bottle to the door. A single tear trailed down her cheek as she knowingly played out her eternal punishment once again. Weakly, Deirdre called out.

"I'm coming, Mother."

FAMILY TIME

"You know this morning when Dad was torturing me?" Simon asked his grandmother.

"Yes, dear. What about it?"

"I don't know. It seemed like his heart wasn't really in it, you know?" Simon's grandmother shook her head.

"No. What do you mean?"

The boy studied the kitchen table. Gram watched his face as he struggled to find the words.

"Well, take this for example."

He held up his left hand, indicating the bandaged index and middle fingers. "He only pulled off two of my fingernails. And even then he didn't dip them in salt or lemon juice or anything. Just bandaged them up."

"That is a little unusual."

"I know, right? Then, when he was taking the scalpel to my feet, he barely scratched them before he stopped."

Simon lifted his wrapped right foot and pointed.

"See? It's barely seeping. I haven't had to change the bandage once." Simon's grandmother patted his injured hand then gave it a good squeeze.

He winced and smiled.

"I'll go talk to him, Sim. Don't you worry. I'll have him back to bleeding you like Jack the Ripper in no time."

"Thanks, Gram."

Simon reached out and back-handed her across the face. She smiled, picked up a fork, and stabbed it into the back of his hand. Gram left him laughing in pain and went to talk to her son.

She found him in the garage, standing next to an industrial-sized table saw. He flicked the switch up and stared at a cobweb in the corner as the blade revved up its melodic screech and shot sparks in all directions. He flicked the switch down, defeating the electric monstrosity without so much as a glance in its direction. He heaved a loud sigh.

"What the hell is wrong with you, Gerald?"

Gerry flinched, then turned his head to look at his mother.

"Jesus, Mom. You scared the fuck out of me."

Gram walked to her son and punched him in the stomach.

"Gerald Anton Bennington, how many times do I have to tell you not to take the Lord's name in vain?"

Gerry doubled over, wheezing and trying to reclaim some oxygen so he could respond. She took this chance and grabbed the remaining patch of hair on his balding head and pulled up. Raising her leg, Gram slammed Gerry's head down until she felt the cartilage of his nose crack against her knee cap. That forced the air back into his lungs and he screamed.

"Dammit, Mom. Fuck!"

As blood poured down his face, Gram folded her arms across her chest. "Now, are you going to tell me what's bothering you or do I have to pull out my scrotal clamps?"

"Nothing is wrong, Mom."

"Oh, really? Then why is Simon in the kitchen, worrying his little ten-year- old heart out about you, his father, who couldn't even manage to make his son cry like a little bitch this morning?"

Gerry blanched. "Did Simon say that?"

"He did. He's worried about you and so am I. This isn't the first time you half-assed a session either."

"I know. I just, I don't know what to do, Mom."

Gerry wept into his hands. His sobs shook his whole body and Gram's heart broke with each hitch and wail. She maneuvered him to a low workbench and forced him to sit down. As she sat next to him, she rubbed her hand across his back.

"What is it, son? You know you can talk to me about anything." When he was able to control his crying, Gerry looked up at her.

"I think Marian has been with another man."

"You think or you know?"

"I don't have any proof, if that's what you're asking. But I can see it. Something's different. She stays out later, showers more often than usual, even when she's not covered in blood and feces. Hell, half the time she won't look me in the eye when I tie her up or take the straight razor to her ears."

He started to cry again. Gram patted his back as she looked around the garage. A jar of salt water sat on a shelf behind her and she grabbed it. She unscrewed the top and when Gerry looked at her again, she threw the liquid in his face.

Gerry coughed and sputtered, wiping at his face in a futile attempt to clear the stinging fluid from his eyes and nose. She threw the jar to the concrete floor where it shattered into dozens of jagged prisms. She picked up one of the largest shards and held it to Gerry's throat.

"I did not raise my son to be a whiny cry-baby pussy. Nor did I raise him to judge a situation or person without all the facts. Did I?"

"No," he gasped. "No, you didn't."

"You're damned right I didn't. Have you talked to Marian?"

"Well, no. Not exactly."

She moved the shard from his throat, then pressed it into the soft pocket of flesh beneath his right eye.

"Not exactly? Either you have or you haven't, Gerald."

"I haven't! I haven't!" he yelled.

Gram lowered the broken glass. She put a finger under his chin and forced him to look at her.

"Would you like my advice?" He nodded.

"Talk to her. You can't let this fester in your heart. You keep this bottled up and the next thing you know, you'll just be another suburbanite with a nine-to- five job and a white picket fence who plays golf on the weekends. Is that what you want? Because it'll happen. Mark my words, if you don't clear up this mess between the two of you, you'll both end up in that kind of shame spiral."

"You're right, Mom. Thanks. Maybe I'd better talk to Simon, too, huh?"

Gram smiled and shoved the glass shard into Gerry's shoulder. As she ground it deep into his flesh, he laughed. He wrapped his hand around hers, forcing the jagged glass deeper.

"What would I do without you, Mom?"

"I shudder to think. Now go."

She yanked the shard out of Gerry's shoulder, pulling down then up, inflicting as much pain as possible. Her son's eyes misted with emotion and he bent back her wrist, snapping the bones with one swift motion. She'd never been prouder.

Gerry walked into the kitchen and found his son sitting at the table, trying to flay the skin from a piece of chicken. They couldn't afford to practice on live animals every day, so Gerry bought bulk packages of meat every week from a nearby warehouse store. But after the way he had let his son down this morning, Gerry thought a trip to a local small animal farm might be a nice treat.

Simon glanced up as Gerry entered but never made direct eye contact before returning to the task before him. Gerry felt a pang of pain in his belly.

"Simon?"

"Yeah, Dad?"

"Look at me, son."

Simon put down his skinning knife and looked at his father. His face was a thin paper mask, barely covering his concern and disappointment.

"I'm so sorry about this morning."

His son mumbled "'s'okay" under his breath. Gerry moved closer then pulled him out of his chair. He folded the boy into his arms, crushing as much air from Simon's lungs as he could.

"No, it's not okay. I wasn't there for you today. I get so wrapped up in my own little world that sometimes I forget about those people closest to me and what they need. Can you ever forgive me?"

Simon tried to wheeze out an answer but Gerry was squeezing too hard. The boy nodded his head as best he could. Gerry released him and the boy smiled with blue lips. A few tiny blood vessels in his left eye had burst and a small dot of red expanded as Gerry smiled back.

"Thank you. You're too young to get involved in my problem now, if there even is one. But I promise, one way or another, I'll straighten it out and then give you an extra special session later. Sound good?"

"You bet, Dad. That'd be awesome!"

He stomped on Gerry's bare foot, mashing the baby toe under his heavy athletic shoe. Gerry screamed with laughter then punched his son in the nuts.

"I'm going to go talk to your mother."

Simon gave him a thumbs up before vomiting onto the linoleum floor. He then collapsed into the spreading pool of bile and what looked like chunks of raw chicken skin.

Gerry found his wife in her sewing room. It had originally been set up as a rec room, but it turned out this family's idea of recreation included more than foosball and big screen TV's. What Marian could do with a little needle, some twine, and human skin was nothing short of art. This room had become her studio, so to speak.

Her back was to Gerry as he entered so she didn't realize he'd come into the room. He watched her for several minutes, admiring the lines of her arms, the muscles of her back as they flexed, and the quick glimpses of her profile as she reached for whatever tool she needed. Just as she pulled back on a long burly line of twine, Gerry cleared his throat.

Marian yelped and swiveled in her chair at the same time. She clutched a hand to her chest as she tried to catch her breath.

"Holy shit, Ger. You scared me. How long have you been standing there?"

"Just a couple of minutes. I love to watch you work."

She let out a nervous laugh then cleared her throat. She wouldn't look him in the eye.

"So, what's up?"

"We need to talk," he said as he eased the door closed behind him. Her face flushed a dark crimson.

"About what?"

"You already know, don't you?"

A tear escaped the corner of her eye and rolled down her cheek. As her chin trembled she wiped it away.

"I...I'm so sorry, Gerald."

She burst into a flood of tears. Heavy sobs wracked her body and she covered her face with her hands. Gerald had trouble understanding her muffled confession so he pulled a box of various textured threads off the only other chair in the room, set it on the floor, and dragged the chair next to Marian. After sitting down, he reached for her hands and pulled them toward him. Her cheeks were a splotchy patchwork of red and swollen skin.

"Marian, just take a deep breath and start at the beginning."

She wiped her nose on her sleeve and took a few calming breaths before she spoke.

"Six months ago, R&P hired a new Ad Director, Jack Smith. About a month later, he and I were assigned to the same project team for a new client. He was handsome and funny and liked all my jokes."

Gerry swallowed the lump of anger burning the back of his throat. He needed to rein in his rage to allow Marian enough time to tell the whole story. If he didn't, he'd have her locked in the Iron Maiden with an army of fire ants, a gallon of honey, and an oversized wasps' nest (shaken, not stirred). He patted her hand instead.

"Go on."

"Well, we started having lunch a couple of times a week. If any work needed to be done after hours, we'd volunteer. We flirted and bantered innuendos about for weeks. Then one night, it just happened."

Marian stared at Gerry, her eyes puffy and red, her mouth turned down in an arc of guilt and shame.

"What happened, exactly?"

She paused before she answered.

"We slept together."

Gerry blinked. He could feel his forehead crinkle. "And?"

"And what? We had sex, Gerry. Isn't that enough? I just wanted to know what it was like, you know? 'Normal sex'. No razors, no nipple clamps, no harnesses or zippered masks. Just your basic missionary position, lights off sex."

"How often did you—"

"Oh God, just the one time. It was awful. I'd never been so bored in all my life. I thought maybe if I tried it more than once it would get better, but I could never bring myself to sleep with him again."

"What else?"

"What do you mean?"

"Well, you've been coming home late, taking a lot of showers. You two must be doing something together."

"Oh, Gerry, no. No, my darling. After that one time, I told Jack it was a mistake. I tried to avoid him whenever possible. I stopped going to lunch with him but he kept pestering me. When he wanted to 'work late' I said I had to get home to my family. But I was so ashamed to face you that I went anywhere else I could think of: the library, a bar, the bowling alley."

"Bowling?"

She laughed. "Yeah. Then when I managed to get

home, I showered to wash the guilt off me. I swear I thought you'd be able to smell it the second I walked in the door."

"So, you just had sex with this guy one time?"

She nodded and stared at the floor. Gerry had never felt so relieved and he burst out laughing. Marian looked up at him and frowned.

"Why on earth are you laughing, Gerry?"

"Because you only slept with another man."

"I'm not following."

"I thought you were going to tell me that you met someone else who was a better torturer than me. That you were going to take Simon and run off with this guy, snatching up victims all along the coast and leave me here all alone."

"Oh, Gerry. I'm so sorry. I was such a fool, thinking I could find anyone or anything better than you and our life together. Can you ever forgive me?"

He wiped the tears from her cheeks then brushed his thumb across her lips.

Her eyes begged forgiveness so he slapped her face, a red handprint rising to the freckled surface of her skin in seconds. He grabbed a fistful of her hair and yanked her head back.

"I don't know. You've been a very bad girl, haven't you, Marian?"

He pulled her hair again and her sharp intake of breath was one of excitement, not pain. They smiled at each other. He pulled her up and out of the chair then crushed his mouth against hers. She accepted his passion and even offered her tongue. Gerry bit it twice, drawing blood.

He pushed her away as an idea formed in his mind. "What is it, Gerry?"

"This guy, Jack. He married?"

"No. He's single and lives in one of those ridiculous lofts downtown. Why?"

"Well, I figured before we rekindle our romantic relationship, maybe we should kindle something else first."

Marian's mouth curled into a feral smile. The blood from her tongue smeared over her teeth, making her appear more savage than a parent trying to push her way through a throng of people to buy a high-demand toy at Christmas. He'd never felt so aroused.

"Like Jack's flesh?"

"Exactly."

"We have to be careful, Gerry. He's not a stranger. He's my co-worker."

"He's only been linked to you professionally, as far as anyone knows. I bet we can get Gram and Simon to help snag him, somewhere particular just to him."

"Hmmm. I think he said he goes to a gym every Wednesday night after work, near his loft. Silver's Fitness Gym on Main."

Gerry looked at his watch and smiled.

"That gives us four days to plan our attack."

Marian wrapped her arms around his waist and snuggled against his chest.

"I love you, Mr. Bennington."

"And I love you, Mrs. Bennington."

She reached under Gerry's shirt and raked her nails along his back. He winced with pleasure then leaned down to bite her shoulder and she giggled.

"I'm going to spend the rest of my days making up for my mistakes, Gerry. Starting with Jack."

"I don't know. Maybe part of your punishment should be to make you watch as Mom, Simon, and I have all the fun."

"But I'm responsible for bringing him into our lives. I should be the one to take him out."

"I suppose you have a small point there."

She laughed. "Small being the operative word."

"You mean?"

Marian held up her pinkie and wiggled it. As they both shared a good guffaw over Jack's short comings, Gerry's Mom knocked on the door.

"Hey, what's going on in there?"

"C'mon in, Mom."

Gram pushed open the door and she and Simon stood in the hallway.

"Everything is okay now, huh?" Simon asked.

"It's better than okay, son. We've got an idea for a new session and we need your help."

Simon's eyes lit up with eagerness. "A family session?"

"You bet. Me, your Mom, you, and Gram. Everybody's going to have a part to play. You up for it, sport?"

"Yeah!"

Simon ran into the room and threw his arms around both his parents.

Gram shuffled in, holding her wrist against her chest, and joined the group hug. "Didn't I tell you it would be all right?"

"You sure did, Mom. Thank you."

The four of them enjoyed a quiet moment of family togetherness as they stood wrapped in each other's arms. Then Gerry pulled away and poked Gram in the eye, ripped Simon's right ear halfway off, and punched Marian in the gut.

"All right, Benningtons. Let's go. We've got work to do."

J esse, along with her best friend, Lizzie, walked into the Secretary of State's office on a bright Thursday morning. Jesse had just turned eighteen on Tuesday and was anxious to get her driver's license. Up until a few years ago, she could have gotten her license at sixteen, but when a rash of fatal accidents involving sixteen- and seventeen-year-olds swept the nation, the law clamped down. That was all right with her. She figured it just gave her a few more years of practice.

The two girls stood in line behind other young hopefuls. A group of them, including three from their training class, were waiting to take the written and driving tests. The written exam came first, then the driving test. Jesse supposed it helped people to calm their thoughts and think through all the regulations and rules before actually getting behind the wheel of a car. There had been a lot of changes in the driving laws in the past decade. At least, that's what her mom told her.

While they waited, a nasally whining voice came over

the loudspeaker: "Security—Pick up in Testing Area. Security to the Testing Area please."

Jesse and Lizzie both turned to the right and watched two large burly men in dark blue uniforms exit from a cherry red door at the back of the building and walk briskly to the front. They pardoned and excused themselves through the lines of waiting people to the far left-hand side of the building where two rows of desks were lined up—the Testing Area. The Testing Manager was the one who called for them and she pointed at a small whimpering man clamped into one of the front desks.

Each desk was made of steel with a retractable chair that could move as far back or as close to the desk to fit each individual person who sat in it. It locked in place once the person began the test and did not unlock until the test was graded. If you passed, the chair automatically moved away from the desk after the Testing Manager entered your score into the computer. If you failed, retractable clamps sprung out from the arms and legs of the chair and held you in place until the Security Team arrived.

Lizzie nudged Jesse in the ribs. "Check it out. What a loser."

Thin, balding, and trembling in a puddle of his own urine, this man had apparently failed. If this was his first attempt at getting a license, they would be lenient. He'd only have his legs or arms broken to ensure that he didn't go out and drive without a license. Then he could come back next year and try again. If this was his second attempt, they'd put him in the hospital for a few months after a ten-minute beating. That was the limit. The original limit was twenty, but after five people died they cut it in half. If you were lucky, you'd live, but you'd never be able to apply for a license again, at least not in this country.

One of the Security men pulled out a wide metal cylinder, about 4 inches long. Jesse thought the guy was about to start the beating right there but it was actually the key to open the locked desk. Once unlocked, the Security team hauled the man, now hysterical and crying, back to the cherry red door and disappeared behind it.

"Five bucks says they show up exactly at the end of the beating," Jesse held up her money and waved it in front of Lizzie.

"You're on. I say the loser's gotta wait at least five minutes."

Through the back alley, a special pick-up area connected to the security office where the failures were held. On an average day, an ambulance showed up four times to the Secretary of State. Ten minutes later the ambulance drove past the front doors and around to the back of the building.

"Ha!" Jesse crowed triumphantly. "Hand it over."

Lizzie slapped the five dollars into her friend's hand. "You're just lucky, that's all."

"Hell no, I'm not. I just happen to know everything."

"Oh really? If you're so smart, then tell me all you know about The Ram." Jesse moved up one place in line as she ran over the details in her head. Every intersection, even the T-junctions, had large steel barriers hidden underground. If you failed to stop at a red light or stop sign, a motion sensor triggered those barriers to roll up from the ground in front of and behind your car to keep you from fleeing the scene. Once the police arrived and wrote their report, they called in for The Ram.

"The Ram's like an old-fashioned steamroller but with a souped-up engine. The roller part doesn't actually roll. It's a large stationary cylinder of concrete about three feet in diameter, six feet across and about six inches off the ground. After the cops catch the offender, they enact a real-life accident.

"See, if you run a light or a stop sign, you're likely to get broadsided. So depending on what road you were on and the average speed limit there, The Ram will drive right at your car at that speed, and the offender is given a few seconds to react, just like in a real accident. If you were driving on a road with a 25mph limit, The Ram would come at you at that speed. If you were on a 50 mph road, blah blah blah."

At the lower speed limits, the driver is usually lucky enough to walk away with a sprained neck and a mostly totaled car. If it's any faster, well, Jesse didn't think the odds improved with speed. Of course, if you did survive, your license was revoked for at least a year.

"Hmmm. Very good. I didn't know that part about how fast The Ram moves."

"Wanna run through some stuff? It'll help us both to remember everything for the exam."

Lizzie nodded. "Don't they do the same thing at the train tracks?"

"Yep. It could be for anyone who tries to run the warning lights or drives around those barrier arms. They just let the train do the dirty work, instead of The Ram. Remember when we saw that car get totaled a couple of years ago?"

"Oh yeah. What were we, like 14? We were riding our bikes in the grass alongside the tracks at the edge of town. I'll never forget"

Jesse was lucky enough to see one of those accidents acted out. She was 14 and she and her friend, Lizzie, were riding their bikes in the grass alongside the tracks on the outskirts of town. Just as they crossed a road and were riding on the grass again, they heard the screeching of tires and gears knocking loudly as the barriers rolled up. They stopped and turned to see a bright yellow '99 Volkswagen Beetle trapped between the barriers and stopped directly on the tracks, in the path of the oncoming train.

Jesse could see a lone woman in the vehicle. Her face was ash grey and her mouth was hanging open. She looked at Jesse, her eyes pleading for help, but the young girl didn't move. You didn't have the option to react if you took on a train. If you tried to exit your vehicle, you were shot on sight. If anyone tried to help you, they were shot. Jesse wasn't sure why the regulations regarding the trains were so strict. Her dad had complained once about the government trying to regulate all the train routes ever since that terrorist group had blown up almost half the railroads ten years ago. Maybe it had something to do with that.

The cop on the scene barely had enough time to sign his report when the train struck the car. Sparks went flying everywhere. The sound of screeching and crunching metal was deafening and Jesse clamped her hands over her ears, but she never took her eyes off the car. The conductor of the train didn't even apply the brakes until after he'd hit the Beetle and dragged it about 100 yards. She strained her neck to keep the car in view as long as possible. Once the train rounded the bend and the car was no longer visible, Jesse turned to Lizzie and gave her a high five.

The nasal voice boomed over the loudspeaker again and broke her reverie.

"For everyone in this line waiting to take the written driver's exam, please pay attention. I'm breaking you into two groups. Will the first ten people in line please come up to the counter? Thank you."

Jesse was the 13th person in line and would have to wait for the first group to complete the test. This would give her a bit more time to mentally review everything she needed to know. She watched the first group line up in front of the Testing Manger and, after they received a stapled pile of papers, mill about the desks and sit down. About half of the group looked pretty confident. There were a couple of guys, though, that were really sweating. They chewed their fingernails down to the quick as they struggled with the test.

Jesse tried to remember all the other violations that she knew you had to list somewhere on the written test. If you drove for more than one mile with your blinker on and did not complete a turn anywhere, you automatically had one point added to your record. The distance said blinker is left on with no turn directly correlates to how many points are put on your license. If you do not use your signal at all, that is also one point. If someone is in the fast lane on the highway but is driving under the speed limit for more than five miles, he gets an automatic revocation of his license for one year.

Those, of course, were the lenient regulations. Jesse tried to think of the more harsh ones. She ticked them off on her fingers casually as if she was mentally checking off a grocery list. Anyone caught driving with an expired license or without any license at all receives an automatic death penalty. She'd never seen it but she overheard her mom talking to one of her bowling friends on the phone.

Apparently, some guy from her own neighborhood had his license revoked for running a stop sign. A few weeks later he was stopped for speeding. How he could have driven with a broken leg and collarbone, Jesse could not figure out. The reporting officer was only going to club him once in the head for the speeding offense but when the man couldn't produce a license, the officer had no choice. He pulled out his service revolver, a nickel-plated .44 Magnum Smith with a 10-inch barrel, held it to the man's temple and pulled the trigger.

Anyone driving by and gawking at an accident, or at someone who's simply been pulled over, is a violation. Jesse was in the car with her uncle when he slowed down to stare at some woman who had been pulled over for speeding. He had his tires shot flat by the reporting officer, and then he had to pay for the cost of towing his car and replacing the tires. The resulting traffic jam he caused by his disabled vehicle added two points to his record. Worse would have been if her uncle had caused an accident. If that happens, the gawker is physically removed from his vehicle, his license is revoked permanently, and he spends a few months in the hospital after three days of torture conducted by the Traffic Flow Regulators. The TFR's did a pretty good job of moving things along. No one wanted to mess with those guys.

Anyone who causes an accident, aside from a gawker, on either highway or side road, gets it the worst. Jesse's Driver's Ed instructor showed an hour long film on penalties for driving violations and this one stood out in her mind the most.

The offender has his license revoked with no possibility of reissue and his car is destroyed. In the film, this man had to stand there and watch as a huge wrecker rolled up to his vehicle and crushed it beyond repair. Of course, the guy still has to continue to make payments if he owes money on it or leases it. Once that's done, the TFR's pick up the man to perform 12 torture sessions, one a month, with high probability of permanent damage. The man in the film had to endure being whipped with a cat-o-nine tails, having his arms skinned, and his penis mutilated.

If anyone, besides the offender, dies in the accident, all of the above applies, except the torture session. The offender then must be put to death in the same manner as how the victim died. In the film, one young boy died in an accident between a Ford Escort and a Chevy Tahoe. The driver of the Chevy was speeding and ran a red light, slamming into the Escort on the passenger side. The boy was in the front seat at the time and the Chevy hit with such force, it crumpled the smaller vehicle underneath it. The boy had been trapped under the dashboard of the Escort for four hours with crushed legs and ribs and a severe concussion. He slowly bled to death before he could be rescued.

The driver of the Chevy was taken to a special facility, had his legs and ribs crushed by a concrete weight and his head bashed in with a police baton. He was then crammed into a 4' by 4' box, with ragged metal edges, covered in broken glass, and left to die.

Jesse shook her head and looked around as the Testing Manager once again whined over the loudspeaker for the remaining people to approach the counter and get their tests. She looked over the group and realized the Security Team hadn't been called. She caught the gaze of one of the nail biters and smiled. He half-smiled back in relief and then threw up. She grimaced at him and then turned away to grab her stapled packet of papers. When she turned back and wove through the desks, she made sure to avoid the spreading pool of vomit. As she sat down, she took a deep breath in through her nose and released it through her mouth as the chair adjusted itself to accommodate her. She was confident and sure of herself and knew she would pass the written exam. Her only worry was the driving test. She hoped she didn't make any mistakes then because she had a hot date tonight. She wanted to wear a cute little off-the-shoulder sweater and didn't want a taser burn on her neck to mar her perfect tan.

S he stared out at the street through the front window. A flurry of snow fell from the sky. Clinging to every exposed surface, it smothered the outside world with quiet. The wind caught the fat round flakes as they fell, giving them the appearance of floating goose feathers.

That type of snow is fragile and soft in its beauty. No craft store glitter or Hollywood special effects could compare to its genuine sparkle, or capture even a fraction of its delicate elegance. She imagined it not to be snow at all but magic dust sprinkled from the tiny satchel of a woodland fairy. The sodium street light on the corner heightened the natural beauty as the orange-yellow glow flashed through the icy crystals, creating small jeweled prisms that dotted the lawn, the sidewalk, the air itself.

A soft tapping on her leg disrupted her reverie. She looked down to see the slender reptilian fingers of Emma's hand, twitching like a tiny flickering flame. Maggie wished the bullet would have taken her daughter's life, but her aim had faltered, and now Emma lay cradled in her lap, jerking and spasming. Blood ran down the side of the couch and pooled into a sticky blotch on the carpet. She stroked Emma's auburn hair, matted thick with blood and feathers, and whispered reassurances to her.

"Sshhh. It's all right. Everything will be all right now. You'll see." Emma's chocolate brown eyes widened, the yellow vertical irises seeming to stretch beyond the limit of their tiny orbs. Those eyes once saw the awe and amazement of the world, as only an eleven-year-old could. Sorrow and darkness had replaced that wonder not so long ago. Now they filled with terror. Her slender jaw, filled with rows of needle teeth, worked open and she coughed out a spray of blood. Maggie could feel the tiny droplets freckle her skin as she blinked against the onslaught of fluid. Within moments, Emma rolled her head to the side and lay still.

Maggie wept. Not in sadness or guilt but in relief. It was over now. No more pain. No more fear. She glanced over at her husband's body sprawled on the living room floor, already stiff in death. He'd never be able to experiment on her daughter again, just as Emma wouldn't have to live with the nightmares from his evil deeds anymore.

She looked out the window again as she stroked her daughter's cheek, or what remained of it. The red and blue roller lights of two police cars lit up the front yard. The snow fell and danced in these new pools of color and, in that moment, lost all its magic.

Maggie cocked the hammer of the .32 caliber pistol and placed the barrel under her chin. She laughed, even as she cried, knowing the horror would soon be over for her, too. Forever.

"Everything will be all right now."

The blast echoed through the stillness of the house.

PUBLICATION HISTORY

"Secretary's Day" First published in *Sinister Tales, Volume 2: Issue 2*, 2007

"Cabin Fever:"First published at *Delirium Webzine* 2002

"Mulligan" First published in the anthology *Elements of Horror*, 2010

"Bad Touching" First published in *Erie Tales V: Dreadful Delusions*, 2012

"Earl" First published on-line at *The New Flesh*, April 2010

"It's Not What You Think" First published in *Erie Tales 666*, 2013

"Here There Be Monsters" First published in Static Movement's anthology, *Closet Monsters*, 2011

"The Lonely Corridor" First published in *Erie Tales 1: Tales of Terror*, 2008

"Keeping Up With the Joneses" First published at *Planet Relish* webzine, 2001. Published in podcast, *Nightmare Fuel*, 2009

"I've Got a Secret" First published in *Erie Tales IV: Tales of the Apocalypse/Resurrection Mary*, 2012

"Manah Made Evil" First published in *Adwenia's Recurring Nightmares*, 2015

"Honor Thy Mother" First published at *House of Pain* website 2000

All material except "Black Rain" and "Reborn" appeared in an earlier version of *Hell Hath No Fury* published by Hazardous Press.

Hell Hath No Fury previously published by Dragon's Roost Press.

Peggy Christie is an author of horror and dark fiction. Her horror fiction/art collaboration with Don England, *Plague of Man: SS of the Dead*, can be found through Amazon; multiple short story collections, as well as her novel, *Primordial*, from Dragons Roost Press; and her vampire novel, *The Vessel*, from Splatter Theater Press. Peggy is one of the founding members of the Great Lakes Association of Horror Writers, as well as a contributing writer for the websites of Cinema Head Cheese and Malevolent Dark. Check out her webpage at themonkeyisin.com for more information on her other publications and appearances.

Peggy loves Korean dramas, dogs, survival horror video games, and chocolate (not necessarily in that order) and lives in Michigan with her husband and their dog, Willow.

Primordial

After being unemployed for too long, Charlie lands a job at a local advertising agency. Once there, she accepts a position on the Secretarial Council, only to find that the secretaries don't answer to human laws and ethics. They worship an inter-dimensional creature, who stumbled into our world eons ago, to get everything they want through sex, fear, and death.

Now Charlie must figure out how to stop this creature from wreaking havoc and chaos throughout humanity before it's too late.

Dark Doorways

Enter this dark mansion of ghastly delights. Each dark doorway opens to another tale of horror. Some rooms are large banquet halls, others are tiny servant's quarters. Each contains wondrous, fear inducing words from master scribe Peggy Christie. If you have the courage, take hold of one of the latches, open the door......and enter.

Forever Trapped

It sits alone at the edge of a cliff, the sea raging beneath it. An easy target, the abandoned home becomes the latest conquest of a reckless burglar. No one will care if he slips inside and takes a few long-forgotten things.

However, this house is not empty. It's filled with lonely souls, souls who only wish to feel alive again. And once they trap the intruder, they will share the stories of their lives with him. Forever.

DRAGON'S ROOST PRESS

Dragon's Roost Press is the fever dream brainchild of dark speculative fiction author Michael Cieslak. Since 2014, their goal has been to find the best speculative fiction authors and share their work with the public. For more information about Dragon's Roost Press and their publications, please visit:

http://www.thedragonsroost.biz